Pit Bulls
in a Skirt

Pit Bulls in a Skirt

MIKAL MALONE

Dafina BOOKS

Kensington Publishing Corp.
http://www.kensingtonbooks.com

DAFINA BOOKS are published by

Kensington Publishing Corp.
119 West 40th Street
New York, NY 10018

All Kensington Titles, Imprints, and Distributed Lines are
available at special quantity discounts for bulk purchases
for sales promotions, premiums, fund-raising, and educa-
tional or institutional use. Special book excerpts or cus-
tomized printings can also be created to fit specific needs.
For details, write or phone the office of the Kensington
special sales manager: Kensington Publishing Corp., 119
West 40th Street, New York, NY 10018, attn: Special Sales
Department, Phone: 1-800-221-2647.

Dafina and the Dafina logo Reg. U.S. Pat. & TM Off.

ISBN-13: 978-0-7582-7468-7
ISBN-10: 0-7582-7468-8

First Kensington mass market printing: August 2012

10 9 8 7 6 5 4 3 2 1

Printed in the United States of America

This is dedicated to Cartel Publications
fans everywhere.
We love you!

Acknowledgments

I'd like to thank all *Pit Bulls in a Skirt* fans who kept this storyline alive through word of mouth. It means the world to me. We hope you show the same support for the movie.

Mikal Malone, aka T. Styles

E-mail: authortstyles@me.com
www.facebook.com/authortstyles or T. Styles Fan Page
www.twitter.com/authortstyles

If you make it through the gates that house "Emerald City," one of Southeast D.C.'s deadliest housing projects, you'll run into four females with colorful ski coats and designer jeans. And if you don't belong, you'll quickly find out what they have hidden in the Marc Jacobs or Louis Vuitton purses they hold closely to them, because these females aren't just pretty faces. They are the women taken out of their beds and placed on the throne by the hustlers they love.

This is their story. . . .

Chapter 1

The Hustlers' Ball

December, Friday, 10:30 P.M.

Mercedes

It had been an hour since I hung up with my mother, and I was still pissed.

I couldn't believe she waited until the last minute to tell me she couldn't watch her own grandkids! Tonight was the wrong night for her to pull this bullshit on me. Mr. Melvin's yearly Christmas party, which we call "the Hustlers' Ball," was in an hour, and it was obvious I wasn't gonna make it.

Mr. Melvin, the property manager, started the parties at the community center in Emerald City to try to stop the violence. However, what he didn't realize was all he did was breed every hustler in D.C. that was in the game. It was the only time we allowed the security guards to open the gates for outsiders, but not without checking the list we provided for them first. We owned Emerald City and everybody in it. Nobody made a move without clearing it with us first. Even though D.C. government paid the guards, they received their *real* orders and *real* money from us.

With five buildings and twelve floors in every one of them, Emerald City was one of the largest projects in the city. Originally named the Frederick Douglass Housing Projects, the project acquired the nickname of Emerald City because all of the buildings had emerald green awnings.

Tucked behind the gates of Emerald City were Murry's food store, a barbershop, a beauty salon, and an arcade—everything you needed, including every kind of drug you could imagine.

"Ma, are you sure you can't watch them for me?" By now, I was begging my mother—something I normally don't do. But for the Hustlers' Ball, it was warranted.

"I'm positive. Bye, Mercedes!"

Click.

She hung up on me! I cannot believe she hung up on me! Man! I can't stand her sometimes!

I opened my bedroom door and walked into the living room. I started contemplating whether I should ask my son, who was sitting on the couch playing a video game, to watch his sisters for me. Asking Cameron Jr. was almost as bad as asking my mother. He had his own mind now, and that was somewhat scary. He was growing up very fast. I knew it was just a matter of time before he wanted in the game and in the life he'd been raised around.

Big Cameron already had him counting the cash we collected at the end of the week from the runners. And as long as he learned the ropes from his father, I had no problem with him dealing when he was ready, but he had to be *ready*. I loved this life and everything about it. Considering the power, the money, and the look on my man's face when he came through the gates and saw shit was still intact, this life excited me. There is no other feeling that can compare—outside of the way Cameron makes me feel when we make love.

"Li'l C, you sure you don't wanna make two hundred dollars tonight?" I asked him while he was playing *Madden* on our fifty-inch plasma-screen TV. "It'll help your momma out a lot."

I sat down and put my arm around him. He looked irritated, and I could tell he knew I was trying to butter him up.

"Doin' what, Ma?" he asked, never taking his eyes off the game.

"Watchin' your sisters," I responded, playing with his hair.

He looked at me with his big eyes and that beautiful curly hair like I had just asked him to do the worst thing in the world. Letting me know he wasn't going for it.

Cameron Jr. was thirteen years old and helped me out a lot with eight-year-old Chante and four-year-old Baby Crystal, but lately Chante was becoming too much for anyone to handle. And I made a promise not to force him to watch his sisters unless I was handling business, and I always kept my promises.

"Come on, Ma! All Chante gonna do is get on my nerves when you leave! She makes me sick sometimes! She cries the moment you go, plus she don't listen."

"Calm down, boy. I ain't gonna *make* you do anything. But you know the ball's tonight, and your Aunt Stacia and Dex gonna be here in a minute to pick me up."

Truthfully, I could've paid anybody to watch them, but I like them to be around their own things and in their own place. Plus I didn't trust just *anybody* in my apartment. And most of the muthafuckas I knew, who would have jumped at the opportunity to earn two hundred dollars for four hours, were fucking with that shit. So sending my kids with them or letting them watch them at my place was out of the question.

Between all of our clothes and our expensive furniture from overseas, I had over $200,000 worth of shit in my apartment. We did real well with the money the drug life gave us, so I didn't need anybody taking it from me because I messed around and let someone in my apartment who could later plot to rob us.

"If I say 'no,' you gonna be mad?" he asked.

"How can I be mad at you?" I rebutted. As I looked into my son's eyes, it never ceased to amaze me how much he looked like his father. "I'm just gonna be upset, that's all." I continued hoping he'd change his mind.

"Well, I don't wanna do it," he said, continuing to play his game and avoiding my stare.

"All right, then," I said, walking slowly to my room. My tired attempt to give him time to change his mind. "Let me go tell your aunt the bad news."

I walked to my closet, which held Cameron's and my clothes. It was so packed that I could hardly find anything when I wanted it. Looking at the packed closet, I let out a frustrated sigh. I would be so happy when Cameron became a lieutenant, so we could finally move out of Emerald City. The bottom line was this: No matter how much money we had, we were still living in the projects. I knew it, even if the people around me chose to forget.

I grabbed my white Eddie Bauer ski jacket and zipped it up all the way to the top. I was just about to leave my room, until I remembered to grab my Marc Jacobs bag with "My Bitch" tucked inside it. My Bitch was the nickname I gave to the nine millimeter. I never left my house without it. I hadn't had to use her yet, but I was willing to . . . if need be.

I walked toward the elevators. As always, the

stench that met my nose reminded me of how nasty my neighbors were. I could immediately smell the dirty apartments and the trash, which sat behind their doors for far too long.

While waiting on the elevator, Derrick, one of the grimiest niggas on my squad, walked up to me. Derrick was a hard worker, but he had a tendency to try me from time to time. I was constantly putting him in his place. At first, I used to tell Big Cameron when Derrick got me wrong, but Cam started getting mad. He said that they'd never respect me if I kept running to him over everything they did. So I started handling stuff on my own, and I only came to him about the big shit.

"What up, Mercedes?" he asked as we both waited on the elevator.

"Nothin'." I did my best to keep my tone even, reminding him that we weren't friends.

"You goin' to the ball tonight?" he asked, still trying to spark up convo.

We stepped into the elevator and I met his stare with one of my own.

"Look." I paused. "You know I'm not with the small talk and shit. So unless we talkin' 'bout business, we ain't talkin'."

"Yeah . . . uh . . . I know," he said as we walked off the elevator. He looked all salty and shit. "I'm just tryin' to be cool with the female I report to, that's all."

I didn't respond. I let him walk ahead of me

because I hated people walking behind me, especially somebody as grimy as Derrick. When we approached the exit to the building, I saw my girls on the steps.

Shit! They gonna be blown like shit wit' me.

Before he walked outside, I remembered I didn't find out the status of the dope fiend who gave him fifty dollars in counterfeit cash in exchange for some of the purest heroin in Southeast.

"Derrick!" I yelled before he pushed open the building's door. The cold air hit my face quickly before the door slammed shut again.

He turned around and walked over to me. "Yeah."

"What happened with that head? You handle it?"

"Yeah." He smiled as he smoothed the side of his face with his right hand and grabbed his chin. "We handled that shit. I think his funeral was last week."

"A'ight, but next time, get back with me."

"Yeah . . . okay." He stopped, clearly still upset that he had to take orders from me instead of Cameron, even though it had been over three years now. "I'll try to remember that."

"You *will* remember."

He nodded his head and turned toward the door. When he walked through it, the night air hit me hard. It wasn't a match for my Eddie Bauer jacket, but it was hell on my jean-clad legs. You'd think by now I'd be used to the cold air, since I had to man my post for twelve hours a day for the past three years.

The first thing I saw when I opened the door were tight-ass cars driving through the gates. *Damn! Rashawn from New York really did get the Lamborghini! She's a lucky muthafucka!*

There were all types of high-end cars navigating the streets. Mercedes-Benzes, which happen to be my favorite, BMWs, Range Rovers, Bentleys, and Acuras flooded Emerald City's gates, heading to the ball. Some playas had gone all out, showing up in chauffeured Navigator and Hummer limousines. Seeing the cars got me horny, and now I was even madder at my mother. For a second I even contemplated *making* Li'l C watch his sisters. But like I said, I never break my promise.

I saw my girls handling business as usual, in designer dresses and fur coats, while waiting for Stacia and Dex to scoop us up. The community center was a ten-minute walk because EC was so big, so we were better off driving, which only took about two minutes.

I laughed when I saw them dressed up while handing out orders in front of the building. And as always, Yvette was the loudest.

"*Look* . . . don't tell me you got it if you don't, Dramon! If shit ain't right when we get back, you might as well leave town. I'm not fuckin' around wit' you!"

"I got it, Yvette," he said, with his hands in his pockets, shaking his head with confidence. "Y'all ain't got shit to be worried about tonight. Me and my soldiers holdin' shit down."

Most of our soldiers were between the ages of sixteen and twenty-one. Cameron said Dex liked them that way because they showed respect; and above all else, they were hungry for that money. He said the older they got, the more rebellious they became and wouldn't take kindly to women giving them orders. Once they reached that rebellious age, he'd cut 'em off. However, if they were good, he'd put them to work outside Emerald City. He wanted as little distractions for us as possible. I respected his plan, but Yvette didn't give a fuck. She was ready to handle them no matter how damn old they were. And most of the soldiers, if not all, *feared* or *respected* Yvette. She could handle shit with the best of the men.

While Yvette was briefing the soldiers, the others turned around and saw me standing there not dressed for the occasion or the night.

"What you doin'? Why ain't you dressed?" Kenyetta asked as she looked me up and down.

I had to give it to my girl. She was killing a red dress, Fendi heels, and the red-and-black lace mink Fendi purse to match it. Kenyetta was five-seven, with dark, pretty skin and Indian hair, which fell to the middle of her back. Tonight she had it up in a classy bun. Men killed for

11

Kenyetta, but she belonged to Dyson, one of the members of the Emerald City Squad.

"Yeah . . . what's up wit' that, Cedes?" Yvette asked after finishing with the workers, who were now at the bottom of the steps manning the gates. "Go put your shit on. Dex and Stacia will be here in a minute," she continued as she pulled out her compact to check her lipstick.

Yvette wasn't the prettiest—but with the money she earned, and the power she had, she quickly became one of the most wanted women in the projects, along with the rest of us. She was a shortie with big titties and a phat-ass to go with it. We joked all of the time about her being one sandwich away from being overweight. She hadn't always been that way. I guess running Emerald City's gates and leading the soldiers took its toll on her body. She had a smooth amber complexion, and sported a short, spiky haircut. Her hair was always fierce, regardless of what she had going on.

At five feet five inches, she was the meanest bitch you could ever come across. I gave the soldiers leeway on *certain* shit, but Yvette didn't give them any on anything. She was in charge of security and made it clear that she wasn't the one to be fucked with, skirt or not. She would carry any nigga anywhere if the money was fucked up or if they were caught slippin'. Being the baddest bitch, it was only fitting that she fucked with the meanest nigga of the Emerald

City Squad. And Thick was the only man who could handle her.

When he came into the room, you couldn't help but respect him. Even the scar on his face made you wonder about the life he led.

"Don't start with me. I'm mad enough as it is," I said, brushing off their comments. I wasn't in the mood to go into what happened with my two-faced mother.

"Don't start with you? Bitch, tonight is *our* night! This is the only night we get recognized for the shit we go through in EC! Ain't no otha project, outside of Emerald, being held down by bitches!" Carissa insisted.

Carissa was usually laid-back, but not when she felt passionate about something. She looked just like a young Salli Richardson, only better. Her skin was the color of copper, and she didn't have a flaw on her body. Not even a mole. She wore her hair in a jazzy bob, which brushed her cheeks every time she moved. She was beautiful.

The niggas gave her the most shit because she was short and cute; and when they saw her, all they thought about was fuckin'. But just like we all dealt with members of the Emerald City Squad, Carissa was no exception. She was messing with Lavelle. And the niggas around here knew if anybody loved their woman, he did. He wouldn't have a problem putting two to the heads of any niggas who disrespected him or her.

"Go and get dressed!" Yvette insisted. "Stacia just called and said she'll be out front in a minute. They comin' through the gate now."

"I can't roll, y'all. I'm serious," I said, tucking my hands back inside my warm pockets. "My mother can't watch the kids tonight."

"Please say you playin'!" Yvette yelled. "Damn! Call her! I'll see if she'll do it for me."

"Don't waste your time. I tried offering her four large and she still said no."

"So you ain't playin'?" Yvette asked in disbelief.

"Naw, I'm not playin', but I wish I was. She messing with Mr. Brown again and she think I don't know that shit. You know his wife's out of town this week at that Mary Kay convention."

"Mom's wrong as shit," Kenyetta said, shaking her head.

"Tell me about it. But y'all go ahead. Just tell me how it was," I said, trying to hide the fact that I really didn't want them to go without me. We did everything together. And I wanted to see if they would ride or die with me for real.

"Look . . . why don't you let Tina watch 'em?" Yvette suggested.

She already knew the answer to that, so I don't even know why she let it fall out of her mouth.

Tina and her badass kids lived with Yvette from time to time when her mother, who lived across the hallway, put her out. Regardless, there was no way in hell I was letting her watch my kids. Besides, Yvette's apartment was nasty and too junky for my taste. The last time I let Crystal stay over Yvette's, she came back with bumps all over her arms and face. I think they were roach bites, and I was mad as shit with Yvette. I got over it after a while, but I made a promise that it would never happen again. Yvette's my girl, but she could take better care of her crib. I'm surprised Thick's big ass ain't put her in her place yet.

"Naw, I can't do that. You know I like Li'l C to be at his own house, around his own things."

"You spoil those kids rotten!" Kenyetta said. "And Li'l C damn near runnin' the place." She giggled.

Before we could get into anything else, Stacia and Dex pulled up in front of the building in his silver Hummer. Stacia looked beautiful. Her white fur coat was the first thing I saw before her glossy lips started moving.

"Party night!" she screamed through the open window.

"No, she didn't get the white mink I wanted!" Carissa said. "Dex stay lacing her up!"

"I know. Don't she look beautiful?" I added, trying to hide the fact that I was slightly jealous.

The cold air blowing through the window pushed her long hair into her face and teased her fur coat. Her honey brown skin was flawless. She was so beautiful that no one questioned why

15

Dex chose her. We walked down the steps and by the soldiers who were already guarding Emerald City.

"Hey, baby!" I said as Stacia jumped out and gave us all hugs.

"Hey, you!" Stacia yelled back.

Dex came around to the passenger side to open the doors for us and we hugged him too. Stacia and Dex was livin' it up for real. They were the Beyoncé and Jay-Z of Emerald City and we adored them. Their relationship was the example we used when we talked to our men. They all made promises to move us out of Emerald City, once we got things tight, but Dex had kept his promise to Stacia.

Stacia and Dex used to live here in Emerald City until he became the chief in command and started pulling in six figures a month. Although Dex got put on and eventually moved, he didn't stop showin' love to the rest of us.

He was here so much that we started forgetting he even moved with Stacia to their eight-bedroom castle-style home in Alexandria, Virginia.

Dex showed his loyalty, but Stacia was another story. She used to come by all of the time to sit with us on the steps of Unit C, like we did before they moved from the projects. We could talk to her about anything—from our relationships to our dreams. And if Stacia could make it happen or help us, she would. She always had the answers. When she left, it kinda hurt. Our group had been dismantled, and it hurt even more when she stopped coming around as much. Dex started getting kidnap threats about Stacia, and he told her to cut the visits short. Sometimes she didn't listen.

Instead, she'd just dress down so people wouldn't recognize her if they saw her sitting with us. But the moment anybody saw the fifth girl posted up in front of Unit C, they'd know exactly who she was, no matter how she tried to disguise herself. We all missed Stacia but understood that Dex kept his promise. We wanted her to be happy.

Dex didn't always have it that way. At one point he ran hand in hand with my boyfriend, Cameron, Dyson, Thick, and Lavelle. But after Dreyfus, our supplier, came in blasting on Tyland Towers, a project a few blocks over from ours, Dex came up with a plan that sealed his position as the man of Emerald City.

They say Dreyfus is six-three, dark-skinned, with smooth black hair. But no matter his looks, he was ruthless. He didn't get involved with every little detail that happened in the projects and hated being bothered with bullshit. The only thing he demanded was his money be right and on time, *every time*. About three years ago, the crew over at Tyland Towers failed to heed his warning.

When some stickup kids from uptown D.C. got the inside scoop from somebody on the inside as to where the warehouse was in Tyland Towers, they took full advantage. They got into the crew for over $200,000 in cash and product that night. And all of that shit was on consignment. When Dreyfus found out that Jamal, who ran Tyland Towers, let some niggas get into him for that much cash, he came through with ten niggas blastin' on Thanksgiving Day.

He killed off all of Jamal's troops and sliced his throat in front of his pregnant girlfriend, Patricia. Then he called a meeting with the captains from all of the spots he supplied. Dex went to represent Emerald City because there was no lieutenant at that time. While they were there, Dreyfus reminded them of his policies, particularly not having his money fucked with, using Tyland Towers as an example. He vowed that shit would be worse if it happened again.

After the meeting Dex came up with the idea of the gatekeepers. He called Cameron, Dyson, Thick, and Lavelle, also known as the Emerald City Squad, and told them about his plan. Instead of them hating, they put the plan into action to ensure what happened to Tyland Towers didn't happen to Emerald City.

The plan consisted of four gatekeepers running the largest unit, Unit C, at all times. Since all of Emerald City could clearly be seen from Unit C, one responsibility of a gatekeeper was to handle "the approach."

The approach happened the moment the security gave the wave that something wasn't right with whoever was coming through. Two people handled that function. The other person handled security and the fourth handled the collection of the funds.

Dex's plan worked so well, that Dreyfus made him the chief of Emerald City. But when the money really started flowing, it became difficult for the EC Squad to man the gates alone. More fiends were coming through, which meant more product and more responsibility. They hadn't anticipated what would happen if things worked out so well. Because of that, they never trained anyone else on the gatekeeper plan, since they didn't trust anyone.

That's when Thick came up with the plan to put us out there. Since we were around them all of the time, they trusted us and we knew Emerald City inside out. That was three years ago, and we've been manning the gate ever since.

"Wow, girl, you wearing jeans?" Stacia asked, tugging at the loop on my belt. "That's different."

19

"I'm not wearing jeans. . . . I can't go," I said, avoiding the disappointment on my friend's face.

"What? Why?" she asked, looking at Dex, who looked more and more like money every time I saw him. The diamond earring in his right ear was so bright that it almost looked like a flashlight.

"Damn, girl! Does your man know that? I just saw him and he ain't say shit about that," Dex asked with his raspy voice.

"Not yet. I can't find him anywhere. You know how y'all take all day to get ready for the ball. He put more time into tonight than he did on me." I laughed. "Well, look, go ahead and have fun!" I didn't want to continue to throw a pity party outside of Unit C and bring everyone down. "I'll be a'ight."

"We can't leave you," Yvette said. "You know that shit. How we gonna go to the Hustlers' Ball with one of the gatekeepers missin'?"

"But y'all look so nice. Seriously, y'all can go without me." I really wanted them to stay and chill with me, but I knew how bad they wanted to show off their outfits.

"Naw . . . we chillin' wit' you tonight!" Kenyetta said as she hit my arm. "But damn, girl, I was gonna kill them in this dress tonight!" She pouted. "Dyson woulda been mad at my ass when I came through them doors. He needs to be thankin' you," she continued as she opened her fur coat revealing her red dress. I could tell that if you shined the right light on it, you would've been able to see right through it.

"You? I wanted to show mine off too!" Carissa opened her coat, revealing her short black Missoni dress under her fur coat, which cost over two grand. "They wasn't gonna be ready for what I was gonna give."

"Well, since we're having a fashion show," Yvette said, "I was gonna kill 'em in my dress too." Yvette's white-on-white look made her look sexy and sophisticated. The full-length fur coat set off her Emilio Pucci dress gracefully. They all looked like a million bucks. And for what? To stay home. "Anyway . . . go ahead, Stacia. We'll see you later."

"Well, okay, guys!" Stacia sighed. "I hope y'all know you're breakin' my heart. How you gonna leave me with the guys alone?"

"You can handle 'em." Carissa laughed. "And keep a close eye on my man."

"I'll try." She laughed back. "I'm gonna call y'all tomorrow!" Stacia said as Dex hugged us, then opened the door for her. "Don't forget about the cookout and bring my babies! *All* of them, Mercedes!"

"Okay . . . I will." I waved.

"I have a surprise for them too," she continued to say as she jumped into the truck, and Dex got behind the wheel. "I love y'all!"

"We love you too! Have fun!" We waved as they drove to the party.

"Sorry, y'all. I know how bad you guys wanted to go," I said, happy they decided to stay. I figured the least I could do was get them high. "Well, since we got the soldiers at the gates tonight, let's crack open the Ace of Spades I have in my apartment on chill. Plus Big Cameron left me a phat-ass J too," I said as we walked up the steps.

"I'm wit' that shit!" Carissa said, smiling.

"Me too," Yvette added, linking her arm with Kenyetta's. "As long as we got each other, I'm good."

Even though we didn't make it to the ball, we still had a nice time laughing and talking about old times.

We were still up at four in the morning when the phone rang. No one expected to hear what we did when I answered the phone.

And the news would change our lives forever.

Chapter 2

Burying Friends

December, Wednesday, 10:37 A.M.

Yvette

It was the worst day of all of our lives.

We were watching our men carrying the caskets of Stacia and Dex, walking them to the hearse that would later take them to the place where they would be buried. Everyone was still in shock, mainly because of how they had been killed. The way it went down was scandalous. Someone had hid in the back of Dex's truck, escaping detection by the gatekeepers. Whoever did it knew that no one would be inspecting Dex's truck and used that to their advantage. It was against *our* law to inspect a squad member's car or stop them at the gate.

They sliced Stacia's pretty face over thirty times before stabbing her in the stomach. And what they did to Dex was unreal. Those muthafuckas actually partially severed his head from his body. They stole all their jewelry, including the diamond earring that Dex bought the moment he became the man of Emerald City. But they didn't just take the diamond out; they actually ripped off his ear. Because of how they did them, we all knew it wasn't just a robbery. The shit was personal, but no one knew why. Dex and Stacia were rich, but they were good people, helping anybody they could.

Through it all, I couldn't shake the fact that if we would've gotten into his truck the night of the ball, they would've been burying all six of us.

Li'l C not watching the kids had probably been the best thing that could've happened to us. I'm happy Mercedes ain't believe in breaking promises to her son.

There were so many people paying their respects that we had to relive the funeral four times that day just to allow everyone a chance to say good-bye. All you saw were dudes dressed in jeans, white T-shirts, Timberlands, and blazers. There were flower arrangements everywhere, including one in the shape of Emerald City, Dex's Hummer, and every kind of gun imagin-

able. Two gold-framed pictures of Dex and Stacia faced the crowd.

The girls and I did our best to hold it together until the last funeral session. Due to the
way they had been killed, all of the services were
closed casket. Hearing and seeing the different
ways other people felt about two people we considered family punched us in our stomachs
every time. With every tear shed, and cry heard,
we were broken down. It was like we were soaking up their pain, and trying to find a place for
it in our hearts.

Our men did what they could to console us,
but they were going through it too. But being
tough like they were, they wouldn't allow it to
show. There were too many people there, most
of which they didn't want to face later if they
were seen crying.

I couldn't help but feel responsible. And although no one said anything to me yet, I felt
fully responsible. I knew that eventually I would
have to answer on how they got through Emerald City's gates undetected the night of the Hustlers' Ball.

*I was in charge! Shit! Why didn't I just go back out
on post instead of drinking?*

I just hoped that Thick wasn't angry with me.
I hated letting him down.

"You okay, baby? Don't worry 'bout this shit!
We handlin' it!" Thick said as he pulled me to
his crisp black suit and squeezed me tight.

There was nothing better than his strong hugs and deep, dark voice to soothe me. I wanted him, right now. He made me feel safe. Suddenly I felt bad for being turned-on, considering we had just buried our friends, but I couldn't help myself. I loved everything about him. Especially the feel of his thick dick when he moved in and out of my body, the way he fussed at me when he felt I was being weak, and the way he always came to my rescue, when I needed him. I couldn't wait until we spent our lives together, and he kept his promise to pull me out of Emerald City for good. And I was patiently waiting.

"I'm fine. I want you to know that I'm gonna find out who did this, Thick," I told him as he released me to look into my eyes. He wiped the tears off my face with his large, rough hand.

He looked down at me and said, "Baby, what you talkin' 'bout? Me and my niggas got this! We know this ain't have shit to do wit' you holdin' shit down in the EC. I just want you to be a'ight so you can do what needs to be done tomorrow. Shit is gonna be business as usual in the city, and we still have an operation to run."

"But this is my fault."

"Yvette!" he said, grabbing my shoulders. "Don't worry 'bout this shit! I got this! Believe dat! I need you to keep focused. If them muthafuckas woulda merked me, I would've expected you to be tough and be on post the next day. This is business."

The thought of *ever* losing him hurt.

Thick leaned in and kissed me. My body melted into his as I inhaled his scent.

"You comin' home tonight, baby? I mean . . . I know you been busy and all, but I really miss you."

"I'll try, baby," he said softly. "But you know wit' shit bein' tight now, me and the niggas gotta handle all of Dex's business and collect debts from a few folks who owe him. *Truthfully,* daddy may not be able to play house for a little while."

My heart dropped and I tried my best to hide my disappointment. But lately Thick hadn't been coming home like he used to. I felt bad for reaching for his attention, using the death of my friends as a reason, but I needed him home. I tried everything I could think of to make him come home more often. I fixed his favorite meals, cleaned up the house when I could, and even stopped fussing at him 'bout dumb shit, but nothing seemed to work.

We had been living together in Emerald City for six years; but over the past year, he'd stay with me once a week, if that. As far as I knew, he didn't have another place, so I hated thinking about where he was staying. Whenever I asked him, he'd tell me he was in and out of New York handling business so he'd stay in hotels. I hoped it was true, but I knew in my heart it wasn't.

I rubbed my hand over the scar left on his

face from the car accident a few years back. For some reason it turned me on even more. His chocolate-colored skin and six-foot-four body earned him the nickname of Thick.

"I understand, baby. But don't forget about me. . . . *Please* don't forget about me."

"How can I forget about you, Yvette? You know that shit ain't possible, but I need you to be strong."

"I'm tryin' to be strong for you, Thick, but I don't know how much more I can take in EC. I want to be with you. I'm ready."

"You know now is not a good time, baby." He sighed, and his voice was heavy with irritation.

"I know, Thick, but me and the girls been training niggas on the side, so we can be ready to leave when shit finally takes off for us."

"Don't tell me you can't handle shit!" His voice was deep and his facial expression changed. I could tell he didn't like the idea of me preparing without him.

"I *can* handle it, baby, but—"

"I know you can," he cut me off. "You wouldn't be out there if you couldn't handle shit."

A few people turned around and looked at us. That's when I remembered we were at Stacia and Dex's house having the repast. Just that quickly I had gotten lost in Thick and our conversation. I missed him so much that anytime he gave me attention, I sucked up as much of it as I could. I wanted every part of it; and if that was wrong, right now, I didn't even care.

"Listen, baby. I'ma get you out of Emerald, but you gotta give me some more time. The only reason shit was easy for Dex was because he impressed Dreyfus wit' the gatekeeper plan.

"We still livin' off his fame right now. Unless we come up wit' somethin' different, all we doin' is seein' plenty of money but keepin' none of it. Just stay wit' me, baby. Shit gonna be a'ight, and then we gonna get that big house we talked about," he said as he reached in for one last kiss before he walked away, taking my heart with him.

I saw Mercedes and them with their men, and I wondered if they were feeding them the same thing Thick fed me. Most of all, did they believe it? The only reason we were strong enough to hold Emerald City down was because of them; and if we didn't have them, we ain't want no part of it, and that was the truth.

I scanned the room and watched grief dwell among the crowd. Slowly the gathering was turning from a somber event to one where people were beginning to find joy in the memories of Dex and Stacia. Just when I thought that things just might be okay, what I saw next ripped my heart to pieces.

Thick was hugging a girl I had never seen before—at least around the hood, anyway. He was consoling her, right in front of me.

Chapter 3

Business As Usual

December, Thursday, 5:45 P.M.

Kenyetta

"You got some more Doritos?" I asked Yvette.

"No, girl. I killed them shits a long time ago!" Yvette said.

"Why you would even ask that girl if she had any more is what I want to know." Mercedes laughed.

"And what the fuck is that supposed to mean?" Yvette said as she stood up from one of the four gray metal chairs that we kept outside. "I just finished 'em."

"Yeah, right!" Carissa stuck her hands in her pockets and tried to stay as warm as the rest of us. "You sucked them down the moment you broke the seal. Everybody know you don't be sharin' no food!" Everyone laughed.

This was the life for us. We were sitting on the

top step watching over Emerald City and the gate. Seven days a week. People made me mad when they said hustlers didn't *earn* their money, and they were just stealing from a weaker group of people. That's bullshit. I wonder if those same muthafuckas could stand outside and freeze their asses off for twelve hours a day, and *still* look as good as we did.

I mean, we were charged with everything: making our men happy and looking good at all times, which meant keeping our hair appointments and wearing fly shit. And most of all, we were charged with being in charge of over sixty niggas, who had a problem with answering to women.

"I miss them, y'all. I can't act anymore like it didn't happen," Mercedes said as she looked at us from under the peach hat she wore with her peach Baby Phat ski coat.

Mercedes was beautiful. Her vanilla-colored complexion and black hair brought out her big, pretty eyes.

"Me too. . . . I don't understand this shit. Dex was paid and all, but he would've put anybody on if they would've proven themselves!" Carissa said as she tied her black scarf around her neck and adjusted her black full-length Eddie Bauer coat. It was obvious she wasn't playing with this cold-ass air, while the rest of us were pressed to look colorful and cute.

"Well, I'ma see if Dramon and them seen anything. I knew we should've stayed out here the moment Mercedes couldn't get a sitter! That was some type of omen or something. That was the sign we needed to check shit out a little further, but we didn't. We all know that we never miss a ball. So why all of a sudden did Aunt Linda say she couldn't watch the kids? I'm tellin' y'all, it was a sign!"

"No, it wasn't. My freak-ass mother just wanted to fuck wit' Mr. Brown. That's why we couldn't go," Mercedes added.

"That may be true, but that wasn't all," Yvette continued. "We shoulda looked into shit a little further, I'm telling y'all!"

Everybody knew that Yvette had been beating herself up over what had happened to them. We all knew she was in charge of security, but she wasn't alone. We all stood right outside that truck and none of us saw those niggas in the back. We knew it wasn't her fault; but being the perfectionist she was, you couldn't tell her that.

"We could've looked into things all day long," I said. "But we would've never seen that shit coming . . . never!"

We were silent for the next few minutes, and I took from that that everyone agreed with me. Dex and Stacia being murdered had taken a serious toll on the atmosphere in Emerald City. For a long time, shit would be real fucked up around here. I just knew it.

* * *

"We don't give a fuck! If you comin' through here, we wanna know where the fuck you goin'!" I said to two girls driving in a green Honda Accord, trying to enter the gate.

The guards hit me on my Nextel and said there was a problem the moment they tried to pull through. They weren't trying to cooperate by giving them the additional information we requested before entering through the gates. Technically, all they *really* had to do was give them the apartment and building number. But the EC Squad wanted the name and affiliation, and these bitches weren't trying to give it to them. As far as we were concerned, they weren't getting through, especially after what had happened to Dex and Stacia. Security was *extra* tight in the city.

"Bitch, who the fuck you talkin' to? I'm comin' here to see my man, and I ain't got to tell you his name or where the fuck he live!" the fat one yelled from the passenger seat.

"Listen, we ain't tryin' to give you a hard time, but if you wanna come through Emerald City's gates, you *have* to tell us where the fuck you goin', or else you ain't gettin' in! It's as simple as that," Carissa said, standing on the passenger side of the car.

"Oh, I know you. You fuck wit' Lavelle," the light-skinned girl said to Carissa from the driver's seat.

"And? What the fuck that got to do with why you here?" Carissa shot back.

"Nothin'. . . . It ain't got nothing to do wit' it, for real for real. I just thought you oughta know that I know Lavelle," she said, laughing a little, like the joke was on Carissa.

"Why the fuck I oughta know that? That ain't got shit to do with you gettin' in this mutha-fucka!" Carissa yelled.

That's my girl! Don't let them bitches know you're moved.

"Listen, bitches, either tell us where the fuck you goin' or turn this raggedy-ass car around! Right now, the choice is yours. But if you keep running your fuckin' mouths, I can't promise you will get to leave this bitch unharmed."

They looked at each other, realizing we weren't playing. Just because she tried to disrespect Carissa, I was more than ready to pull her out of the car and pay fifty dollars to Shaneta and them across the field to stomp the fuck out of these bitches, until Carissa said to stop.

"Okay . . . calm down. We got it," the driver said sarcastically. "Tell them where we goin', girl. After all, we do know Lavelle and he's cool. He *real* cool. I don't want him thinkin' we tried to play his li'l girlfriend," she continued, looking up at Carissa and grinning.

All I was thinking was that if Yvette had been in charge of the approach instead of security, she would've knocked this bitch in her face the moment she said Lavelle's name out of her mouth. Just on GP alone.

"Well . . . *anyway*. I'm goin' to see Derrick in Unit C. He's expectin' me. You can call him right now, if you don't believe me," the passenger said.

"Naw . . . it's cool. But next time just say that shit," I said, giving the security guards the signal to let them in. I should've known these dumb-ass bitches were coming to see Derrick's trouble-making ass. "And stop wasting everybody's fucking time!"

As they pulled off and parked in the lot on the side of Unit C, I wondered what was up with that. What had me messed up the most was the fact they knew Derrick. It seemed to me that he should've warned his bitches about Emerald City's policies. Apparently, he didn't. I knew that Derrick constantly tried Mercedes, and that he had no respect for women in authority. I also knew that eventually we'd have to deal with him before shit hit the fan.

The other thing that was wild was how she kept reppin' Lavelle's name, like she *really* knew him or something. I knew that the moment our shift was over, Carissa would be deep in Lavelle's shit, and I didn't blame her.

* * *

36

The moment Dyson called me and said he would be over, I finished my shift an hour early and drove to my apartment in Unit B.

But when he walked through the door, he slumped on the couch and didn't appear to be in the same lovemaking mood I was.

"Listen, Kenyetta, y'all gonna have to watch everything around here," he said. "With Dex gone, a lot of niggas are gonna try us, thinkin' we ain't got shit tight no more. We gonna be comin' around more to make our presence known, but don't be caught slippin'. Y'all have to really watch each otha's backs."

"And what about the dope testers? We still runnin' them next week?"

"Yeah . . . but make sure niggas play it smooth. I don't trust nobody. I can't believe they took my man! Damn!" he said as he rubbed the side of his head.

"I know, baby. I miss him and Stacia too."

"This shit is fucked up! Why they had to fuck with Dex? He wasn't even that type of dude!" He was trying to hold his tears back by screaming, but it wasn't working. And I was ready to be there to kiss each one that he let fall.

"Don't worry. We got our hands in every-thing. We ain't lettin' shit slide by, baby," I said, trying to reassure him.

"I know you do, baby, but I'm serious. Beware of everybody and everything. With us giving

37

them testers out this week, the gates are gonna be flooded with fiends. We need to make sure everybody's on the up and up."

Dyson was serious, and it scared me a little. Prior to now, he never acted as if he doubted we had things under control. What hurt the most was that although I missed him and needed him to hold me, he was briefing me like I was a soldier and not his lady.

"Okay, baby," I said as I grabbed his hands. "But tonight I need you. I need to be with you. Can you just make love to me?"

He smiled and pulled me down on the couch with him. I had gotten rid of my grandmother earlier and was happy to be spending some quality time *alone* with my man. Lately she had been getting too nosey and asking too many questions. She wanted to know who was looking over this unit, and who was looking over that unit, instead of worrying about her high blood pressure and taking care of her health.

He took off his jacket and I knelt down and removed his shoes. When both were off, I slid off his jeans exposing his crisp white boxers and rising dick. It was just the confirmation I needed, to know that he wanted me.

I slowly lifted up his shirt while kissing him softly on his chest. Then I made my way to his lips and gently sucked them.

"What you doin' to me, girl?" he moaned.

"I'm making love to my man," I told him seductively.

Before going any further, I removed his boxers and reminded him of how vicious my head game was. Slowly and softly I sucked his dick, as if my life depended on it. He ran his fingers through my hair while thrusting softly in my mouth. I knew that no matter what, my sex game could always bring him back to me. At least I hoped.

That night I fucked him in every way he wanted. Dyson had told me that it was my sex game that had hooked him, but it was my heart that kept him.

Although I loved that he appreciated how good I could make him feel, I battled with the idea that another girl could be out there doing the same thing to him, if not better. So I vowed that whenever I made love to Dyson, I would fuck him as if it were the first time, every time. Because in my heart . . . it was.

Chapter 4

Added Drama

December, Friday, 10:38 P.M.

Carissa

"I can't believe you ain't giving Lavelle none of that backdoor action!" Yvette laughed with the rest of our friends. "You better take care of your man, girl, before somebody else does."

"I do take care of him, but ain't nothing wrong with my pussy either," I told her.

"I can't believe you don't like takin' it in the ass, Carissa." Mercedes laughed as she drank from the Hennessy and Coke mixture in her cup.

"That shit is too uncomfortable for me. I told his ass the last time he asked me *not* to ask me again."

"You wild as shit!" Yvette laughed.

"He ain't complaining, though. Trust me."

"I told you what to do, Carissa. You have to

put some bomb-ass music on, get the K-Y Jelly, and tell Lavelle to ease it in *slowly*. You can't rush a dick into virgin ass. You have to be easy wit' it," Mercedes added.

"Naw, I tried that, and it *still* didn't work. I ain't fuckin' with y'all no more. Messin' with y'all the last time, I got my asshole damn near ripped out."

"Trust me, you'll be lovin' that shit before the night is over." Mercedes laughed as she gave the others five.

I couldn't believe my friends were letting their men hit it from the back. They loved ragging on me about how I sexed Lavelle, but he complimented me all the time on the way I handled him in the bedroom. As far as I was concerned, if their men had to fuck them in the ass, something was wrong with them, not me.

We all stopped talking when Critter, the most trusted dopehead in the hood, came running up the steps. Although we liked him, we never allowed anybody to approach us unless it was a resident going into the building, or one of the lieutenants. We stood up and all put our hands on our guns. We trusted Critter; but after what happened to Dex and Stacia, we couldn't give out benefits of the doubt no more. For all we knew, somebody could've given him a bag of dope to smoke us all.

"What up, Critter? You know you ain't supposed to come up here like that," Yvette reminded him with her hand tucked in her coat, holding her weapon.

"I know . . . I know . . . but Derrick won't give me a tester!" he said. He looked bad. The effect the withdrawals were having on his body was evident.

I asked him, "What you talkin' 'bout, Critter?"

"Me and Rod went up to him to cop a piece. He gives him three, and then turns around and tells me to get the fuck outta his face."

"Why he say that?" Mercedes asked.

"He said I got one already."

"So just get one from Rod!" I told him, trying to prevent what I knew was getting ready to happen, which was more drama with Derrick's ass.

"I tried to ask him, but Rod took off running the moment Derrick hooked him up. Y'all know you can't catch no fiend." He laughed, trying to make a quick joke. "Can you please talk to him for me? I ain't feelin' too good."

We all knew why Derrick did that shit to him, but he was being real petty. Although it wasn't the law, he was supposed to be servicing *all* of our customers. Not just the ones he liked, or, better yet, the ones who looked out for us.

Critter was valuable to us when it came to getting the word out to other fiends when we had new product. He was our eyes and ears in places we couldn't or wouldn't dare to go. Because of that, Derrick couldn't stand him.

"Don't worry 'bout it, Critter. We got you," Kenyetta said, turning her attention toward the soldier at the bottom of the stairs. "Hey, DJ! Come up here for a sec."

DJ ran up the steps. "What up, Kenyetta? Want me to carry his ass outta here?"

"Naw, he cool. You got any more testers on you?"

"Yeah, I got a few."

"Well, hook Critter up. And if you see Derrick, tell him we want to talk to him for a minute," Yvette added.

"Cool. Come on, Critter. I'll give it to you down there." DJ knew better than to exchange drugs in our presence, so he was following procedure. We didn't ever want to get caught with dope on or around us and run the risk of being locked up. That would put the entire operation in jeopardy.

"Thanks, y'all," Critter said. "I 'preciate this. If y'all need me to wash your cars tomorrow, bring 'em round front."

"It's cold as shit out here, Critter." Yvette laughed. "Just get us next time or somethin'."

"You got it!" He continued running down the steps.

Derrick was becoming a pain. He couldn't seem to understand that things were the way that they were, and there was nothing he could do about it. It was better to go with the flow, then to go against it. He did everything we told him to do, but in his own way and in his own time. Frankly, he was getting on my fuckin' nerves.

When Derrick walked up the stairs, he already looked like he was gonna give us trouble. His face was twisted with aggravation.

"Derrick . . . why you fuckin' wit' Critter? You know he brings us a lot of business around here," Mercedes asked, shoving her hands in her pockets.

"I ain't fuckin' wit' him. I thought he already had one, and I wasn't givin' him another one."

"Look, Derrick, stop fuckin' with him. Treat him the fuck like you treat everybody else!" Mercedes yelled. "He a customer, just like these otha muthafuckas out here."

"Man, what you want me to do? Give him whatever he wants, whenever he asks for it? We won't neva make no damn money fuckin' wit' his ass."

"That ain't what she saying, Derrick. She saying stop causing bullshit for people who you know look out for Emerald City." Yvette was about to get in his shit for the disrespect. If he said one more word, he could possibly be cut off. "And since you here, what's up with them girls you had comin' through here yesterday? They almost got fucked up for real."

"Man, that's my girl! What you sayin'? Y'all controlling who I fuck wit' too?" he asked, obviously upset.

"We ain't sayin' that shit. What we telling you

is to control your bitches!" I screamed. "Now if you fuck wit' her, like you say you do, I'm sure you want her breathing."

"Whatever."

"Yeah, what the fuck ever! Get back to work, nigga."

He looked back at me like he wanted to kill me. As far as I was concerned, if he wanted to bring it, I was ready. With Yvette and my girls backing me, he would have a hard time. The bottom line was, I was tired of his blatant disrespect to everything we said to him. He wasn't runnin' Emerald City; we were! I made a mental note to tell Lavelle to cut his ass off the moment I talked to him cuz I'm tired of his shit.

Doctanian, one of our lieutenants from Unit A, came up the steps. "Carissa, we five sixty-nine."

That meant they were low on supply; and because shop wasn't closed for another three hours, we had to replenish him. There are five stash houses in EC, one in every building. Since I was going home, anyway, and lived in Unit A myself, I decided to hook him up.

"I'll handle it, y'all," I told them as I zipped my coat and ran down the stairs to my car.

"You want one of the soldiers to go with you?" Yvette asked.

"Naw, I'm good. Anyway, you know the rules. They can't know where the stash house is, so I'll be a'ight," I told them as I walked toward the building.

"You got anything on you now?" I asked Doctanian as I approached the door to Unit A.

"Yeah, we got a little something, but for real we butt naked as shit out here!" he said as he served a head, who was mad that he'd taken a few seconds to give me the status.

"I got you," I told him as I went inside.

Once in the hallway, I made sure no one followed me, or noticed me heading toward the stash house. We made it a point to change them up on the regular to keep people off our track, and to prevent niggas from robbing us like they had done a few years back at Tyland Towers. When I saw the coast was clear, I walked toward the elevator and pushed the button for the fourth floor.

Kristina ran the stash house for Unit A, and only eight people had the key. Originally, it was only the Emerald City Squad. However, since they were away a lot running other shops, they had four keys made for us too. Besides the eight of us, only Dreyfus, Dex and Kristina, who had been working with him for years, knew where we kept our product.

When I opened the door to A46, Kristina, who was sixty years old and had been in the game all her life, stood up and held the end of the gun she carried in the holster. Her fine, thinning hair was pulled tightly into a ponytail, and she had a cigarette in her mouth, like she always did every time I saw her. The apartment looked just like a factory. There were boxes and boxes of empty vials, rolls of glassine paper, and money wrappers everywhere. The other two stash houses looked similar in Emerald City, and were run by other loyal workers too. She managed all of them, but she only worked the one in Unit A.

"It's just me," I quickly told her before she let one loose from her gun.

"Oh . . . Carissa. What you here for? They low already out there?" she asked as she sat down.

"Yeah . . . I need to get a little bit of everything. We closing shop in a few hours, anyway, but they still need somethin' right now. The testers killed us today, cuz they were buying two and gettin' one free."

"If they smart, they would," she said as she put out her cigarette and moved toward the packaged supplies.

When she handed me enough dope, crack, weed, and E pills to last them a few hours, I chilled for a while to make sure no one was on my trail. When I felt I had waited long enough, I stuffed the product in the inside of my Eddie Bauer coat. I looked out the peephole before opening the door.

I was halfway to the elevators when I saw three figures in dark clothes with their hoodies pulled over their heads quickly moving in my direction.

"There she go, right there!" one of them whispered as they ran toward me. "Get that bitch!"

I know this ain't happening!

I can't believe somebody would be bold enough to rob me. They had to have a death wish. With my heart in my throat, I took off in the opposite direction, knowing that it would eventually lead me to the other side of the floor by another elevator. The coat was weighing me down, but I moved as fast as I could. I was willing to bust my gun if I had to, and was prepared to take as many of them with me as possible.

One of them yelled as the other took off in the opposite direction. "One of y'all go the other way, so we can catch that bitch in the middle!"

What was I gonna do now? They were trying to block me in. Constantly checking my back, I was running fast enough to put a nice amount of space in between us. The faster I ran, the more I moved out of their sight. I noticed the janitor's closet, but I didn't go in right away. I wanted them to think I went down the stairwell, so I opened the door and slammed it. Then I turned the knob to the closet and prayed that the door was unlocked. It was!

I quickly but quietly squeezed myself into the closet, then locked the door behind me. Here I was in a closet with over a thousand dollars' worth of shit in my pockets. I knew if they tried to open the door, I'd be dead. And if they decided to fill the closet with lead, there would be nowhere I could run. There was hardly anywhere in the closet for me to move. Not to mention, the smell of the mop bucket filled with soiled water next to me reeked of piss and Pine-Sol mixed.

I tried desperately to stop my heavy breathing, and hoped they would think I went down the stairway, which was through the door directly across from me. When they stopped in front of the closet, I was scared. I covered my mouth when my teeth began to rattle. *Please, God, get me out of this*. I could see them a little through the slots in the door, but not clearly.

Completely out of breath, due to chasing me, they talked in low voices.

"Where . . . you . . . think she went?"

"I heard her run out the door! I hope she ain't seen our faces," the other said.

I tried to see them; but from where I sat, no one looked familiar. The slots blurred their faces. Maybe it was the adrenaline, but my mind was completely messed up. By this time the other guy, who had run in the opposite direction, reached them.

"Where she at?" he asked out of breath.

"We don't fuckin' know."

"Well, let's get out of here before she tells

them Emerald City niggas! Damn! We should've waited for her to come to the elevators!"

"We can't worry 'bout that shit now. Let's roll!" they said before running down the stairway.

I sat in the closet for ten more minutes before moving. I waited until their footsteps completely faded. When they were gone, I called the first person I thought of . . . Lavelle.

"Baby!" I said in between my tears. "I was set up. Some niggas just tried to rob me."

"I'm on my way!" Lavelle yelled through the phone.

Shit was about to get real deadly in Emerald City. I just knew it.

Chapter 5

The Emerald City Squad

December, Friday, 11:45 P.M.

Emerald City

The passengers in the black Ford Excursion 4 x 2 XLS were completely silent. Lavelle, Thick, Dyson, and Cameron were all inside as the sounds of "Hail Mary" filled the air. It sounded as if Tupac himself were riding with them.

At Thick's slide's house, they had already discussed the robbery situation. Thick's slide was a broad out in B-More whom he fucked on the side. They expected niggas to try something sooner or later, but they didn't expect it to happen this soon. And they never expected one of the girls to be the target.

"I'm tellin' y'all, if they would've hurt Carissa

. . . I'da lit that whole muthafucka up!" Lavelle said, breaking the silence.

"I feel you, son, but don't worry 'bout shit. We gonna handle them muthafuckas," Cameron promised.

Lavelle was crushed. He would've murdered everybody in Unit A if something had happened to Carissa. The thought of almost losing her was causing him to lose his temper. Compared to all of the other squad members, he loved his girl the most. He meant what he said when he told her that the moment the money was good, and they trusted and trained someone else to operate the control station at Unit C, he would move her out. This incident made him want to move her out of Emerald City even more. In fact, the only thing he loved more than her was his squad; and in his heart he knew that one day he would have to choose between the two.

When the truck pulled up in front of Unit C, the women let out a sigh of relief. It had been just twenty minutes since Carissa told them what had happened, and already their men were there and on the job. The sparkling black truck and spinning chrome wheels represented safety and a peace of mind to them.

One by one, they all hopped out of the truck, trying to reassure their women that they had everything under control. Just the men's presence alone made them feel better.

"How you doin', baby? They touch you? They ain't put their fuckin' hands on you, did they?" Lavelle asked.

"No, baby! They ain't got me, but I was so scared!" Carissa cried in his arms.

Lavelle and Carissa looked so good together— they easily could have been brother and sister. His Hawaiian-colored skin matched hers perfectly. And right there on Unit C, they held and kissed each other as if it could've been the last time they saw each other.

"You okay, Yvette?" Thick asked. His large and tall body covered hers like a warm blanket.

"I'm fine, daddy. I know you gonna handle them niggas, so I ain't even worried 'bout it." She tried to convince her man she wasn't punking out or nervous at the turn of events. "Just come back to me in one piece."

"No doubt, baby! I ain't lettin' *nothin'* keep me away from this ass," he said, pulling her closer to him.

"I want you to go in the house, Mercedes. We gonna have Derrick and them look over the control station for the rest of the night. We gonna handle them niggas, believe that," Cameron said as he covered her lips with his. "We puttin' shit down tonight, so muthafuckas know we ain't playin' out here!"

But in all of the excitement, all Mercedes could do was cry.

"Come here, baby," Dyson said as he grabbed

Kenyetta. "Shit is all good, so don't even worry 'bout it. Keep my side of the bed warm, cuz I'm comin' home tonight."

In five minutes the Emerald City Squad had managed to eliminate all their fears. But just as quickly as they had come, within minutes they were gone—gone to handle the people who had tried to take from them what they worked so hard to build.

One by one, the men covered in thick North Face, Sean John, and Eddie Bauer coats ran toward the truck with their heat tucked closely against their bodies. Each of them vowed to put as many bodies on their pieces as necessary. Strapped up and mad as hell, they drove to Unit A. Each of them was ready for war.

Chapter 6

The Right Place at the Wrong Time

December, Saturday, 1:18 A.M.

Emerald City

The heroin was coursing through Critter's veins as he sat hidden against the washing machine in Unit A, on the cold, dirty floor. Roaches, ants, and other bugs ran all around him as he injected the heroin into his body. Although he never felt the original feeling from when he first shot dope, he agreed that Emerald City had the purest shit in the D.C. area.

With his head against the dusty wall, he let the euphoria take over his body. He could have easily spent the rest of the night in the same position, until he saw the lights come on in the laundry room and heard several voices. Recognizing CJ's and Charles's voices, he froze and stayed quietly in his position.

"They fuckin' here, man! I'm tellin' you, they know something!" Charles, one of Doctanian's runners, whispered loudly.

"What the fuck you talkin' 'bout, Charles? For all we know, they could be here lookin' for just *somebody*, and not necessarily us. So stop trippin' and shit! You makin' us look hot," CJ said. CJ was also a member of Doctanian's team.

"Well, we have to be cool, but careful too. You think Doctanian know something?" Charles asked.

"Naw, but if we start runnin' and shit, they gonna know something's up. If they even think we had somethin' to do with it, they'll kill us," CJ said.

"I hope you ain't playin', young. Cuz I can't go out like this. You said it was gonna be easy. You said your girl saw them runnin' out the stash house earlier, and that the shit was in there," Charles said, clearly more upset and nervous than the other.

"I know what the fuck I said. Just chill out and stop trippin'. Let's get back out there, for they really start expectin' somethin'," CJ said.

They were almost out the door when they heard movement in the corner. Slowly and carefully they pulled out their weapons and moved toward the sound. They saw Critter laid up against the wall. The dirty shoestring, which just moments earlier had been used to find his vein, was still wrapped around his arm. But Critter didn't move. Like a possum in the woods trying to avoid his attacker, he remained still. He hoped they would think he was so doped out, he didn't hear anything.

"You up, nigga?" Charles asked, holding the gun nervously in Critter's direction. Charles was so scared that he would've pulled the trigger the moment Critter exhibited consciousness.

"That nigga not up! He a dopehead that just got high! Dirty muthafucka," CJ added.

"I say we kill his ass, anyway. We was talkin' a lot of shit in here just now. What if it gets back to them Emerald City niggas?" Charles asked, ready to be the one to do the job.

Hearing this, Critter was so scared that he was almost taken out of his high. Still, he remained in the same state they saw him in. *Dear God, please don't let me die like this. Please don't let them kill me,* he thought. Just like so many other people, he found religion *only* when his life depended on it.

"Do it then. I'm outta here," CJ said as Erick, who was also there, looked on. Before leaving Charles alone, Erick took one last look at Critter.

Charles was just about to pull the trigger, when Doctanian, their lieutenant, approached them.

"Where the fuck you niggas been? The Emerald City Squad is here. Somebody tried to rob

Carissa, and they askin' questions. Meet us in the alley round back."

With that one statement, Charles was gone. But Critter didn't move until he was sure they were out of sight. And as soon as they were, he picked his self up off the floor. He knew the first thing he had to do was tell the girls what he had heard.

Critter was far from stupid. He knew the more they trusted him, the more they looked out for him. This was why the other fiends played him so close. He was the one person they could always count on, to have access to dope at all times. When he felt the coast was clear, he ran out of the laundry room, heading toward Unit C.

Chapter 7

The Basement Apartment

December, Saturday, 2:17 A.M.

Duck Down

"Donald, please stop being nosey! What if they see you?" Latonya asked her boyfriend while sitting on the floor under her living-room window.

"We got the lights out! They can't see shit, but shut up before they hear you."

Latonya and her boyfriend were listening to the Emerald City Squad reprimand six of their soldiers and their lieutenant from Unit A about what had happened to Carissa. Because the members were standing so close to the window, Latonya and Donald could clearly see—even with the lights out—the labels on their jeans.

"Now, what the fuck happened tonight?" Thick

yelled as he walked back and forth, looking each of his soldiers in the eye.

Although no new chief had been named after Dex was killed, it was agreed that Thick would question the soldiers, since his large size automatically provoked fear.

CJ, the youngest soldier on Doctanian's team, spoke. "I . . . uh . . . don't know, Thick. I'm tellin' you, we were out here all night and didn't see anybody runnin' out or following Carissa."

"Well, in order for them to know where she was goin', somebody had to know she was there. Now, she came through the fuckin' front door!" Thick continued as he stopped in front of CJ. "So what you sayin' now sounds like bullshit!"

His plan was working. He had the young workers shook. He felt it was just a matter of time before one of them sold the other out. He wanted to let them know that something *was definitely* going to happen tonight. With Dex being gone, they couldn't take the risk of letting this grave disrespect slide or having it happen again. After all, they answered to Dreyfus, and all he cared about was his money. What happened tonight could have fucked with that.

Meanwhile, Lavelle waited eagerly for the opportunity to bust a cap in whoever was responsible for terrorizing the love of his life. And right by Lavelle's side, with their hands tucked in their coats, were Cameron and Dyson, waiting for the results.

When Lavelle's phone rang, he ignored it. There wasn't anything more important than finding out who had tried to rob them, and hurt his future wife. But when he saw it was Carissa on the other line, he excused himself from the lineup to answer the call.

Under the only light in the alley, his expression turned from that of business to that of rage. His friends noticed the change and immediately knew something was going on. After receiving his information, and ending the call, he slowly walked over to Thick and whispered in his ear.

CJ, Charles, and Erick were on edge, for they realized that it was possible that someone fingered them.

The smell of piss and the rats running back and forth only heightened the feeling of dismay and death. Tonight someone was definitely going to die; it was just a matter of who.

"Somethin' definitely getting ready to happen now, baby," Donald whispered. "These thugs getting ready to kill somebody. I just know it!"

"I wish you would shut the fuck up before they hear you! If you can hear everything they sayin', how you know they can't hear us?" Latonya asked.

"Girl, I know these kinda niggas! Didn't I tell you I used to run Benning Road with thirty muthafuckas on my payroll? These muthafuckas ain't thinkin' about nothin' but handlin' business. They ain't worried about nobody in a window."

"You don't know them. Niggas today kill people for any reason. I think you should just leave stuff alone," she pleaded.

Donald heard her words, but he ignored all of them. The possibility of violence erupting before his eyes excited him. That was one of the main reasons he liked young girls who lived in the projects. It allowed him to relive his past, and to be around all of the things he was familiar with. He used to sling coke and heroin when he was a teenager himself. He was in the game all the way into his late thirties, until he started using coke, instead.

After he fell off, he lost everything, including his wife, their $500,000 home in Upper Marlboro, and his kids. He broke all the promises he made to her, especially the one about opening a business, instead of selling coke. However, he couldn't stop nor did he want to. He loved the power, the respect, and the women too much to settle down. Being this close to danger only reminded him of what he had, while wishing he were still a part of it.

Thick's voice was serious. "Doctanian, I'm gonna ask you one more time, nigga! So you betta think before you open your fuckin' mouth. Did you have an eye on all of your soldiers at all times?"

"Uh . . . yeah . . . but . . . at one point I asked CJ and Charles to get me somethin' to eat. I was hungry from pulling all those hours. You know how it is when those testers come out, man. But otha than that, I had an eye on them the entire time. I swear, Thick. I ain't lyin' to you," Doctanian said, praying that someone didn't include him in whatever happened to Carissa.

He was guilty of being a bad lieutenant, but he was loyal and hardworking; Thick and the others knew it. Doctanian knew that the lieutenants of Emerald City didn't have the same privilege as the captains of the Emerald City Squad or the ladies of the control station at Unit C. They had to be outside, working hand in hand with their crew, only taking brief breaks in between. They were compensated more; but since most of them didn't like serving hand in hand, the extra money didn't give them any real power.

Directly in front of Latonya's window, Jake, the soldier next to the youngest, heard movement in the apartment behind him. He made a mental note to say something when the moment was right. He wouldn't dare say anything now and risk whatever they had in store for someone else being given to him, instead.

"You were hungry?" Thick laughed sarcastically. "You're in charge of a shop, which earns you more money than the president of the United States, and you were fuckin' hungry? Are you serious?

"Let me remind you muthafuckas what the Emerald City motto is. It's 'Honor, Loyalty, Obedience, and Silence.' That's the muthafuckin' creed we live by. Now, I understand that self-preservation is the biggest instinct of any man, but in Emerald City, there's no room for that shit!" he yelled as all six of Doctanian's soldiers stood in fear, wondering what would happen next.

"Let this be a lesson to all of you. Emerald City not goin' for bullshit. Don't sleep. Dex gettin' killed only made us stronger than ever!" Thick emphasized as the members of the Emerald City Squad began to get hype over what he was about to do: murder.

Without saying another word, he walked up to CJ, and said, "You broke the code. Good night, nigga!"

Bang!

The shot from his nickel-plated 9mm entered CJ's head. The others were disoriented for a moment, but they quickly stood back in line as they glanced at one of their members, lying motionless on the ground.

Charles and Erick were petrified. They definitely knew that the possibility was greater now that someone had seen them too. But Erick didn't intend to go out like that. He was ready and willing to bust right back at Thick and anybody else who wanted to kill him, before he just stood still and accepted his fate.

"You can take the next one. He's all yours," Thick said as he looked at Lavelle and faded backward.

Lavelle stepped up from the position he took at the start of the meeting. His movement was so fluid that it appeared he walked on air. Without saying a word, he squeezed two into Charles's face. When Charles dropped, and only when he dropped, did Lavelle resume his position alongside his squad. He was glad Thick hadn't forgotten that he wanted a piece of whoever had tried to kill his girl. Like always, he remembered, and that gave Lavelle the pleasure he needed. Seeing Charles drop was so satisfying, he immediately felt his dick get hard.

I'm not going out like no sucker. Fuck that shit! Erick thought. With his hands behind his back, like they demanded from all of them earlier, he placed his hand in a position that would give him quick access to his 9mm. In his mind his destiny was already chosen, and he was willing to accept his fate. But unlike his co-conspirators, he had plans to take at least three of the captains of the Emerald City Squad with him.

"Now the rest of you niggas get back to work!" Thick said as he saw the only four members left in Doctanian's crew begin to leave.

"And . . . Doctanian!" Dyson yelled.

"Yeah?" he said as he turned around nervously.

"Don't worry, these niggas will be replaced."

Doctanian nodded his head, and then moved out of the alley and out of sight.

But Erick still couldn't believe he had been spared. Whoever gave the message delivered it incorrectly. There were three of them involved in the plan to rob Unit A's stash house. One thing was for certain, the Emerald City Squad wasn't as soft as he thought they'd be after Dex was killed. They were more vicious than ever. He decided to lie back for a while and then resume his plan to rob the stash house later, when he got another crew. And this time he would do it carefully, and leave no witnesses.

When Jake slid back through the door and moved toward the alley, Thick and the others wondered what was up.

"What you doin', li'l nigga? Get back to work!" Dyson yelled. "We got this shit here."

"I am . . . but, uh . . . I wanted to tell you something," Jake said.

Sensing something was wrong, they listened to what he had to say. After Jake told them of the witnesses who could possibly be behind the window, they realized what they had to do. Slowly and carefully they directed their attention to the same window that Jake had stood in front of earlier. Without hesitation they each pulled out their weapons and sprayed the basement-floor window full of holes. They did not stop until they emptied all their clips. Latonya and Donald died instantly.

Pleased with how things were handled, they walked off toward their truck parked on the other end of the alley and drove into the night.

Chapter 8

On the Strength of Love

January, Monday, 3:32 P.M.

Mercedes

"Cameron, you got to talk to your daughter! You know she brought a knife to school last week and almost got expelled."

"Well, was somebody tryin' to fuck wit' her or somethin'? Cuz I ain't gonna tell her not to defend herself, Cedes."

"She pulled it out on the teacher, Cameron. That girl is becoming *terrible*! I'm tellin' you, I might have to get some help for her."

"What the fuck you talkin' about? 'Get some help for her'? My daughter don't need no fuckin' doctor. So if you thinkin' 'bout that shit, get it the fuck outta your head right now!"

"Well, what you want me to do? Keep lettin' her act a fool? I need some fuckin' help!"

Cameron didn't understand that Chante was not innocent anymore. He didn't understand how serious things were with her. It seemed like every time I came in from working the station, my mother would tell me about something else she had done. All Cameron cared about was Li'l C. He never put any real time in with his girls.

"Where's she?" he asked.

"With my mother," I said. "Want me to go get her?"

"Naw. I'll talk to her later. Where's Li'l C? I wanna run him to PG Plaza tomorrow to get those shoes he wanted."

"He's with her too. Li'l C don't need any more shoes. We don't have anywhere to put his shit now." I stopped for a moment and then asked the question I always did when I got my cue. "When we gonna move, baby?"

"Stop fuckin' wit' me, Mercedes. We already talked about this shit. Soon as shit is stable, we'll move. Why you keep askin' me, when you know how tight shit is around here? Niggas just tried to take us down. We can't be moving away."

"But you have been saying the same thing forever, Cameron. With the money we make and what you get from the other shops, we could at least afford a nicer apartment. I'm not saying we have to buy the house I want. I just need more room for all our clothes and stuff. I'm tired of living like this. Emerald City is filthy."

"Filthy? What you talkin' 'bout, Mercedes. You been livin' around here all your life. It ain't like our apartment ain't laid."

"But what happens when we walk out the door? I got to work overtime right now to keep the roaches and rats from otha muthafuckas' apartments creeping over here. I want the life you told me we would have when things got better. It seems like all you care about when you come home now is business."

Cameron stood up from the sofa and walked over to me. I already knew what he was trying to do. Make me forget about what I wanted by making love to me. And although I knew, I still couldn't resist him. His chocolate-colored skin and perfectly sculpted body called me. It didn't help that he was wearing nothin' but boxers and the platinum-and-diamond chain that hung around his neck.

When he finally reached me, he pulled me into him and placed his lips over mine. The scent of his black-box Code cologne by Giorgio Armani reminded me so much of what I needed from him: safety, security, and love.

Unlike my friends, I wanted this lifestyle. But living in Emerald City without being able to escape when I wanted to made me feel no better than Critter or any of the other muthafuckas we served. I liked being a hustler's woman, but I felt I was losing my man. I was supposed to have everything I wanted, including a place free from the fiends and drug addicts, which made us rich. But I didn't.

"Listen, baby. . . . Just give me some more time. We need y'all here cuz wit' people tryin' to take us down, all we got is each otha. There's nobody ready right now to run EC. Niggas are on serious crud time. They just waitin' for that perfect moment, to catch us slippin'. You see how many times niggas tried to rob us since they tried to get Carissa, right? Imagine what would happen if they saw us packin' up and runnin'? I'm sorry, baby, but right now is not the time to leave."

"When *will* it be, Cameron? What about our kids? Don't they deserve better too?" I asked, desperately trying to hold back my tears.

"Yes, they do, baby," he said as he reached in for another kiss and removed my shirt. "Y'all do. As long as I got blood in my body, you'll have everything you want and everything you need."

I don't even remember how we went from the living room to the bedroom, but Cameron did his best to make me remember why I made him my man. From sucking my toes, to kissing my eyelids, he made love to me as if he needed me as much as I needed him. As I slid down on his large eleven-inch dick, I let my body tell him how much I cared for him.

The look in his eyes as he took pleasure from

my wet pussy reminded me who was really in control. Me.

Around and around, up and down, I fucked Cameron like a professional. This was the only real time I had his full attention. This was the only time he let his guard down and gave in to me. We didn't stop making love until we couldn't do as much as lift our heads. And before I knew it, we were fast asleep.

Cameron's ending a call awakened me. I didn't move because my gut was telling me that he was gonna leave again. Ever since Carissa had been set up, they stayed with us night and day. They made their presence known in Emerald City. And after they murdered CJ and Charles, niggas knew they weren't playin'. For two whole weeks we had them all to ourselves; but every time his cell phone rang, I prayed that wouldn't change.

"We gotta go downstairs. Get dressed," Cameron said in a serious tone.

I hustled to get myself together and did a "John Wayne." A John Wayne consisted of washing my face and ass and brushing my teeth in the sink. I knew that whatever was getting ready to happen required my immediate attention, so a bath was out of the question.

I watched Cameron tuck his heat to his body and throw on his thick black coat and I grabbed my big beige coat.

Once off the elevators, the first thing I saw was Thick leaning up against the rails outside with arms wrapped around Yvette's waist. I noticed Carissa with her arm wrapped around Lavelle's as he tucked his hands inside his coat pockets. Finally I noticed Kenyetta and Dyson sitting on the top step of Unit C, looking in our direction. I could tell from the looks on their faces that something was going on.

When I pushed open the building's door, I was nervous. I mean, all of my friends were there, but lately too much shit was happening. But when I was outside, I saw my favorite car glistening. It was the one I had been stashing money aside to purchase behind Cameron's back: a candy apple red Mercedes-Benz C-Class C55 AMG, with a big black ribbon on top of it.

I didn't want to get carried away. But by the way everyone was smiling, I couldn't help but pray the car was for me.

"Baby! Is it . . . Is it really?" I asked him as he smiled at me.

"I don't know. Why don't you take these and find out," he responded, handing me a set of Mercedes keys.

As Cameron gave his boys some dap, I bolted down the steps toward my new ride. My girls quickly ditched their men and were right behind me running down the steps. It felt like Christmas Day. There was no special occasion, and I wondered what I'd done to deserve such a tight-ass present. Once I opened the door, I saw a dozen long-stemmed roses, with a note that read: *Stick with me, baby, and I'll make all your dreams come true. One day at a time.*

Before I could cry, he came down the steps, opened the passenger door, and sat down. I was so overwhelmed that I was speechless. Nothing I could say would express how much this gift meant to me.

He closed the door and I closed mine too. I watched my friends circle around my car, inspecting it from the outside.

"I know shit gets rough, baby. Don't think I don't know. But do you know how good it feels, to have a woman by my side who can hold shit down? I know a lot of niggas who dealin' wit' females who would be scared as shit to do half of the things y'all do out here. I need *you* to know, I appreciate everything you do, ma. I *will* get you out of these projects—the moment we get shit right. But you valuable right now, baby. You more valuable than you realize. We're building a dynasty! With Dex and Stacia killed, we have to watch each otha's backs. Are you wit' me, ma? Can you be that down-ass bitch I know you are?"

I was still trying to formulate words, but I knew my heart and my eyes told him exactly what I felt.

"Yes, baby. I can be anything you need me to be. I'll lay down my life for you, Cameron."

"That's what's up. Wit' that being said, Mercedes Johnson, will you do me the honor of being my wife?" he asked as he pulled out a four-carat princess-cut diamond ring.

"Yes, baby! Yes, I will!" I said as I kissed him.

"You made me the happiest man on earth."

"And you made me the happiest woman!" I kissed him and he wiped the tears that fell from my eyes.

"Well . . . let me let y'all do you. I got something in the glove compartment for you and the girls to chill off, to celebrate. We'll get into the details of our wedding date when you get back."

"Thank you, baby! I love you so much," I said, meaning every word I said.

When he opened the car door, my girls flooded in.

"Girl, let me see!" Yvette screamed as she claimed her spot in the front seat. "Oh shit! Cameron outdid them niggas major, girl! Thick better get his game up." Yvette laughed, comically saying what she *really* felt.

"What you do to Cameron, girl?" Kenyetta asked. "I need to take lessons."

"Yeah, I wanna know too!" Carissa said.

"Well, for starters I take it in the ass." I laughed.

"Fuck you!" Carissa laughed back. "But if it's like this, then maybe I should apply extra K-Y Jelly." We all laughed.

When we opened the glove compartment, I saw three Morning Fresh air fresheners, which were my favorite, and a stack of money.

"Gotdamn, C!" Yvette yelled out the window. "You want two wives?"

"Naw, I'm good." He chuckled on the top of Unit C.

"Don't worry, baby! I'ma do somethin' bigger and better than this nigga!" Thick laughed with his boys.

"I just want you to come home more," Yvette yelled, slightly ruining the mood with her sincerity.

He winked. "I got you, ma."

"I love you, Cameron!" I said, starting my engine.

"I love you more, wifey!"

His show of affection in front of his boys added to my ego. For that moment I couldn't imagine life without him.

As we drove off, heading to Tysons Corner in Virginia, I realized that I was willing to stand by Cameron even if we were on our way to hell. I needed him; and if he was willing to make me his wife, I knew he needed me. At least I hoped.

Chapter 9

Leadership Stricken

January, Monday, 7:15 P.M.

Doctanian

"You know the Lord don't like what you doin', son. You gonna have to answer to somebody sooner or later."

"Yeah, I know, Ma, but right now, I gotta do what I gotta do."

"You ain't got to be in the streets, son," his mother said as her butter-soft hands gently touched his face. "You don't have to do nothin' you don't wanna do, baby."

Doctanian hated when his mother reminded him of his life in the streets. She had been questioning him repeatedly about what had happened to CJ and Charles. He felt she had a strange way of knowing everything. Although he wasn't the culprit, he knew exactly what had happened, and it had been eating him up ever since.

Mrs. Madelyn Bright was an active member in her church, and she hated living in Emerald City. With the money she received from Social Security, she couldn't afford to move. She ran an active "War on Drugs" campaign at church, even though she was unable to prevent what was happening in her own home.

"Ma, look around you. All the food that comes in here I buy. We wouldn't have nothin' if I didn't get out in them streets. If it's not me, it would be somebody else selling drugs to them people."

"But, baby, you got the gift of leadership. You can make anybody do anything you want 'em to do. You ain't nothin' like yo momma. I didn't have nothin' past a sixth-grade education, but you went all the way. Straight A's and all! Instead of leadin' them young men into a life of crime, you could be helpin' them get out."

Doctanian knew what his mother was saying was true, but he was too deep into things now. He had seen too much. How could he turn back now?

Doctanian was twenty years old and had a beautiful golden brown complexion. His six-two height quickly made him appealing to all the girls in EC, but Doctanian was true to only one. That was his eighteen-year-old girlfriend, Jordan.

Jordan had light skin, with beautiful long hair and a distinctive mole on her upper lip. Her body was well developed, and she chose the right clothes to accentuate her thick ass and curvaceous body. From the moment he laid eyes on her, she had him. Unlike a lot of niggas in the hood, Doctanian had a heart. The moment he let her know he ran the Emerald City Squad, she sealed her position by his side by sexing him in ways he never imagined. Although younger than Doctanian, she had way more experience in the sex department. Now that he'd gotten her pregnant, he was even more loyal to her.

"Ma, I ain't nobody's leader. I can't take on that type of responsibility," he said, not realizing that by commanding six men every day, he was doing just that. "I gotta go, Ma. I'll talk to you later."

When he saw the sorrow in her eyes, he said, "I love you, but I'm nothin' if I don't take care of you." He placed a kiss firmly on her face and walked out the door.

"Li'l C, come here, man!" Doctanian yelled as he continued to watch over his soldiers. After being reprimanded the night of CJ's and Charles's murders, he micromanaged their every move.

"What, man?" Li'l C yelled back, letting off the vibe that his father ran the hood, so he didn't have to answer to anyone.

81

"Just come here for a second, man!" Doctanian yelled back.

Li'l C stopped talking to one of Derrick's workers and made his way to Doctanian. He looked so much like his father, Cameron. Whenever Doctanian saw him, he immediately had respect for him.

"What you want, nigga?" Li'l C responded with arrogance. He knew the power his father had, and he made sure everyone else did as well.

"I wanna know why you keepin' time wit' Trey and them?" Doctanian responded. "Them niggas ain't nothin' but trouble."

"No reason! We just kickin' it. Why you in mine, anyway?" he responded as he laced his Timbs and brushed off the little bit of dirt that snuck up on them.

"I'm in yours cuz it's not cool to be out here right now, man. Where your moms at, anyway?"

"She wit' my aunts and them. They rollin' round in her new ride."

"Word? What she get?"

"A new Mercedes!"

"Oh, for real?" Doctanian responded, really feeling happy for her.

"Yeah, but I'm bored as shit!" Li'l C said.

"Well, let's do this. You chill from out here, and I'll see if your pops will let me take you to Dave and Buster's later."

"For real?" Li'l C said as his face lit up.

"For real, li'l nigga!"

Without another word, Li'l C took off toward his grandmother's house.

Doctanian was happy because he liked the li'l guy and he didn't want to see anything bad happening to him. He knew that far too much was happening in Emerald City these days, and it was best that the young teen stayed somewhere safe.

When his tour was over, Doctanian called Cameron and made sure it was cool; then he scooped up Li'l C and they headed to Dave and Buster's in his black Camry. These were the best of times, but the worst of times was sure to come.

Chapter 10
Scared for Life
January, Monday, 9:15 P.M.

Yvette

"Girl, I hope you don't mind me hugging your man when we get back!" Kenyetta yelled from the backseat. "He really looked out with the money he gave us today for shopping."

"Yes, I do mind you hugging my man!" Mercedes yelled.

Everyone got quiet. I couldn't believe she was acting funny already. Hell, they weren't even married yet and already she was acting territorial.

Mercedes started laughing. "But I don't mind you hugging my *fiancé*."

Everyone laughed.

We were out of the parking lot, and on our way back to D.C., when I remembered I left my Tiffany charm bracelet at the store.

"We gotta go back, Mercedes!" I yelled.

"Why? What's up?"

"I left my bracelet in that damn shop," I said, looking into my empty blue Tiffany box.

"Girl! I knew you were gonna do that shit," Kenyetta said. "That's why I told you to put it back in your box after she finished polishing it for you."

"Hindsight is twenty-twenty," I told her.

When we got back to the Tiffany parking lot, I tried to hurry inside to get my bracelet before they closed. But the person I saw coming out the door of the jewelry store stopped me in my tracks. I saw the same girl the day of Stacia and Dex's funeral. The same girl Thick consoled as if she belonged to him. The exact same girl I had several nightmares about, ever since I saw her face.

"Oh . . . hello, Yvette," she said, sounding and looking as if she had seen a ghost.

"Hi," I responded, surprised that she knew my name. "I'm sorry, but do I know you?" I added, hoping she would provide some info about herself, like who she was, and what her relationship to my man was—especially since it was obvious that she knew so much about me.

"I'm a friend of Stacia and Dex's. My name is Zakayla." She smiled as she reached out her hand to me.

"A friend of Stacia and Dex's?" There was no

way she was a friend, because any friend of Stacia's was a friend of mine.

"Yes. I met you at the repast, remember?"

Not only was her presence threatening, but she was also a liar. I never formally met this bitch. I took notice of the diamond rings on her fingers. They were huge and I could tell whoever she was, she was definitely being taken care of. What stood out the most was the scar she had on her chin. I couldn't help but feel a little jealous that she and Thick shared a similar flaw.

"Oh . . . yeah." I smiled slightly. "Well . . . hello, Zakayla," I said, trying to pull myself away from noticing how beautiful she was. "It was nice to meet you again, but I really have to go now. My boyfriend is waiting on me to get back home," I lied. "Maybe I'll see you around."

"Yeah . . . maybe," she said as she walked out the door.

When I grabbed my bracelet from the salesclerk and rejoined my friends in the car, I was out of it. Prior to seeing that bitch, we were having such a good time. I didn't bother telling them about the run-in. Besides, I didn't want them telling me I was trippin'. Not to mention, I wasn't trying to ruin the evening. But still, all I could think about was whether there was something going on between her and my man that I needed to know about.

Unfortunately, the answer had just stared me right in the face, but I wasn't tryin' to see it.

Chapter 11

What About Me?

January, Thursday, 9:22 A.M.

Kenyetta

"That's tight that they're getting married. You think we could ever make a move like that?"

"Baby, stop tryin' to follow behind everybody else. The only reason Cameron is marrying that girl is cuz they got like twenty kids together." He laughed as I helped him pack his clothes to leave me for the weekend.

He and the other captains of the EC Squad were going away to look after the other shops. They had spent so much time at Emerald City that the other places were starting to suffer. We weren't as mad as we thought we'd be because we never expected them to stay so long, to begin with. On a regular basis, out of a week, they came home three days.

"I'm not following behind anybody, baby. It's

just that I know we haven't been together for-ever, but I still want a commitment, Dyson."

"Listen," he said as he threw his packed bag next to the door. "I can't be pushed into doin' nothin'. When I put a ring on your finger, you're gonna know I'm ready, and it won't be four carats like Cam gave Cedes. It'll be a carat for every year we been together."

Looking at Dyson's muscular body made me want him all over again, but what he said about not wanting to marry me got in the way of how I wanted to express that.

"What's wrong with my little Indian girl?" he asked as he pulled me to him. "Did I tell you how sexy you look today? My man was tellin' me the otha day how these niggas be tryin to get at you and Carissa. Don't let nobody come near my pussy!" he said.

I thought that comment was ridiculous. Why would I want the jesters, when I had a king?

"I won't, baby," I said, smoothing my hair back with my hands. "Call me later."

When he walked out the door, I looked through the mail and sat in the living room with my grandmother. She was far too nosey, and lately I'd been doing everything within my power to avoid her.

"Hey, Granny, how you feelin'?" I asked cour-teously.

"Oh, now that your little boyfriend is gone, you wanna stop neglectin' your grandmother.

Well, don't waste your time! If you ain't spend no time with me, then don't worry 'bout me now."

"Granny, what are you talkin' about?" I asked, not really wanting to know.

"I'm talkin' about you sending me away for the past few weeks so you can be a whore!" she yelled, pointing her wrinkled finger in my direction. "And what's this I'm hearin' about Mercedes marrying that Cameron boy?" Without waiting for an answer, she continued her tirade. "All of you ain't nothin' but a bunch of criminals terrorizing what used to be a nice neighborhood."

"Bye, Granny," I said, realizing even more why I shipped her off whenever I got a chance.

I walked into my bedroom and lay across my bed. My mind went through all of the events that happened over the past few weeks, including Cameron's marriage proposal. Maybe Cameron and Mercedes would be the next Stacia and Dex.

I missed Dex so much. He was there when I needed him the most, a little over a year ago, and it was only because of him that I was even still living. I didn't know what I would've done if he hadn't shown up the night he did.

Dyson had just left the house, after threatening to end the relationship again. He had done that from time to time, whenever he wanted an excuse to see other women. My grandmother was gone on an overnight convention at church. Dex had come up to see Dyson regarding a new shop opening up in Oxon Hill, Maryland, but he had just missed him. When he noticed my front door open, he walked in.

"Kenyetta, what are you doin'?" Dex asked me as I sat on my apartment floor with a gun in my hand, preparing to take my life.

"Nothin'!" I sobbed. "Why are you here, anyway, Dex? Your friend broke up with me and left again! I hate my life!"

"Don't say that shit!" he said, staring at me with concern. His eyes were fixed on the weapon.

"It's true! Why can't I make him happy?" I asked as I began to cry harder.

"Kenyetta," he said as he carefully took the gun out of my hands. "That dude may have a lot of shit goin' on, but one thing's for sure. He loves you."

"How do you know? All y'all are probably the same, anyway," I said as he helped me off the floor and to my bedroom.

"What you talkin' about, girl?" he said, flashing the smile I was sure had won Stacia over.

"I'm talkin' about if a girl is not a supermodel type, y'all don't want to be bothered."

"Have you seen yourself, Kenyetta?" he asked as he sat on the chair next to my bed.

"Yes . . . and?" I said, not feeling up for bull-shit.

"And you're fuckin' beautiful! I'm tellin' you right now, if I wasn't fuckin' wit' Stacia, you woulda been my girl a long time ago."

When I lifted up off the bed to look into his eyes, I noticed they had changed from when he first came through my door. For the first time ever, I could tell that Dex, the one man every woman lusted after, wanted me.

"But why? What's so good about me?" I asked, hoping he could convince me that I was worthy of anybody—let alone him.

"Well, I'm a sucker for that soft hair and chocolate skin. It's not often you see a beautiful woman with both. Plus that ass. I'm tellin' you, shawty, Dyson has caught me a few times checkin' you out. You a dime, Kenyetta. It's simple as that. I don't know what's goin' on with you and Dyson, but he'd be a fool not to want you."

I was beginning to feel better. Dex thought I was attractive, but I figured he had to be lying about wanting to sleep with me. He had to be saying all of that just to prevent me from pulling the trigger. But I could tell he was willing to go as far as he had to, in order to save my life.

Lie or not, I felt better about myself, and it was all because of Dex. But now there was an-other problem: I wanted him. I wanted him in my bed and I wanted to feel him inside me. I knew it was wrong to have these feelings. Stacia was one of my best friends in the world. But I needed him . . . just for one night. I wanted to know how it would feel to be with the chief of Emerald City. Above all, I needed to *feel* loved.

My wish was granted when he moved toward the bed and gently kissed me on my lips. His kiss was gentle but passionate—something I'd never gotten from Dyson before. Softly, and as if he loved me, he moved his soft lips all over my face while removing my nightgown.

"I'm afraid, Dex."

"Don't be, baby. Let me love you for one night. Let me show you how you deserve to feel. Let me show you how shit would be, if you were my lady."

With that declaration I gave in to him. His soft sucks on my breasts made my toes curl. When I thought I couldn't take it anymore, he methodically ate my pussy, as if he'd been dreaming of it. For the first time ever, I reached an orgasm through oral sex, and I had Dex to thank.

But what we did next, we would forever be wrong for. He removed himself from his jeans and, without protection, entered my body, which was anxiously waiting on him. That night Dex made love to me, and it was the first time I'd ever made love. He held me until six in the morning; and in more ways than one, he saved my life.

We never talked about it again, knowing what we shared would always be kept between him and me.

To this day I'd always love Dex for what he did for me. And I would never know if he thought about me as much as I did him.

Chapter 12

Just Another Day

January, Sunday, 6:22 P.M.

Thick

Thick was running shit around the south side of D.C.

The shops he started in the areas surrounding Emerald City were quickly making him one of the richest dealers in the area. Thick had another purpose that he wouldn't stop at, until it was complete. That was taking over Emerald City and securing his position as the new chief.

"Why you taking me home now, Thick?" Zakayla asked while his Ford Excursion truck made its way toward home.

"Look, you know what the deal is. I got shit to take care of back in the city. I'll get up wit' you later, baby! Why you trippin'?"

"You sure you not trying to get back to Yvette? I mean, when you gonna tell her about us,

Thick? I can't keep livin' like this. Either you gonna be with me, and work on the family we supposed to have, or you gotta leave me the fuck alone."

Thick hated how women claimed they could handle a man with a double life. Yet, the moment they got feelings, they would start nagging and bothering niggas and shit.

"Look, don't start pressuring me, Zakayla! I don't need this fuckin' shit! I got enough to deal wit' at home wit' Yvette," he yelled in a tone so loud that it rocked his truck the same way his speakers could.

"Who the fuck you talkin' to, Thick? If it's gotta be like that, don't worry about comin' back to me. Shit, I need a man full-time."

Thick couldn't push Zakayla's emotional buttons the way he could Yvette's. He knew that although she loved him, she would've wasted no time cutting off his ass. She already had her ex-boyfriend sneaking around, just waiting for his ballin' ass to fuck up. Zakayla dumped Irvin because he was too weak; and unlike Thick, he didn't know how to handle a woman with her own mind.

He pulled over at a park along Route 40, in Ellicott City, Maryland, a few minutes from the apartment that he put Zakayla up in.

"Listen, I'm feelin' you, and I know you know that shit. But I'm a man, baby, and a man can't

98

be given too many ultimatums. All you gonna do is push me away. Now, you know good and fuckin' well I wanna be wit' you. So stop lunchin' out, when you know I got shit to take care of."

She turned around and faced him—immediately causing him to become humble the moment he looked at her beautiful face. Just moments before, he was narcissistic and full of himself. Everything about Zakayla was beautiful. Her dark complexion and thick, long eyelashes gave her an angelic look. Just looking at her, one would never expect that she was the future wife of a hustler. Thick had planned to marry her sometime next year.

"Okay, baby," she said, playing on the fact that her beauty mesmerized him. "Why don't you put your seat back, daddy. I wanna give you a li'l somethin' to remember me by while you're on the road back to D.C."

Obedient and horny, Thick did exactly what he was told. Zakayla moved her body over his. She was petite, with a size-4 waist, phat ass, and 36-D titties.

Gently she pulled his dick out of his jeans and placed him raw, inside her wet and eager pussy. She wasn't fucking him; she was fucking the power he represented. The life she wanted. She covered his mouth with hers and rotated her hips until he came. Thick thought Zakayla was on the pill; so cumming inside her was a privilege that she offered that Yvette couldn't. If they didn't use a condom, Yvette made sure he pulled out, and Thick hated it.

When Zakayla was done, she sat silently in her seat on the ride home. In her mind there was nothing else to say. She wanted the last thought he had of her to be their sexual encounter. Examining her engagement ring, she felt even more confident that he would go through with everything he'd promised. Since the day he proposed to her, in front of the Emerald City Squad and her friends, she had been planning their wedding.

When they arrived at the apartment, where he paid the rent, he walked her to her door to see her in safely. Back in his truck, he tried to prepare himself for dealing with his other life— all of the while knowing he was nowhere near ready.

Thick didn't have time to shower before he went home to Yvette. And as most men did sometimes, he underestimated how smart his woman was. He came through the door and put one arm around Yvette's waist, pulling her to him. Yvette had one thing on her mind, examining her man to see where he had been, before he was able to jump into the shower.

"What you make to eat, boo?" Thick asked, moving toward their refrigerator.

"Nothin' yet. You want me to make some of them cheddar cheese burgers from Murry's?"

"Yeah, that's cool," he said, irritated that he had to ask her to cook, when she knew he was coming home.

That was another way Zakayla won him over. She took care of him, and treated him in a way that all men loved to be treated. In addition, Zakayla worked out regularly, and she took good care of her body. Lately Yvette had been gaining more and more weight, and the size-10 body Thick had grown attracted to had been replaced with a size 14. With all of that said, Yvette was still cute; and most men around the block loved her thickness, just as much as they loved the way she was able to hold Emerald City down. Thick, on the other hand, was beginning to hate it.

The other thing that made Thick choose Zakayla instead of Yvette as his wife was how they survived a car accident together, which had scarred both of their faces.

One night Zakayla had gone to Love, a night-club in D.C., and had seen Thick blessing the bar with his cash by ordering drinks for everybody in VIP. He had told her that night that he was visiting his sick cousin and couldn't chill with her.

She was even more hurt when she saw a few of her so-called friends taking from the money that was supposed to be in her pockets. They didn't even bother calling her to tell her he was there. What upset her the most was this girl who appeared to be glued to his arm like the diamond-emblazoned Movado watch he rocked. When Zakayla made her presence known, she left the club. Thick quickly followed her, leaving the Emerald City Squad behind.

When they finally made it outside, Thick ran after Zakayla, desperately trying to rearrange in her mind what she'd witnessed.

Walking angrily to her car, she made up in her head that she didn't want to hear anything he had to say. As far as she was concerned, he was disrespecting her. What Zakayla didn't count on was Thick overpowering her and throwing her in his truck.

Without asking, he lifted her up off her feet and put her in his truck. He securely locked her in her seat belt. In spite of the fight she put up, she still ended up in his passenger seat on the way down the road.

Drunk, he took off driving, afraid that he might have lost the one female who excited him since he first met Yvette. Without looking, he ran into another car, which ricocheted and hit his truck again. Thick was thrown through the truck window; and Zakayla, while still wearing her seat belt, received a minor concussion and the scar she wore on her face today. Thick didn't mind being scarred up, saying that the marks they wore brought them closer together. Six months later, he asked her to be his wife.

He never told Yvette the full truth; he told her he was in the truck alone the night of the accident. Catering to his every need, Yvette nursed back to health the man who had hurt himself while confessing his love to another woman.

"Make love to me now," Yvette demanded, trying to see where his head was.

"Naw . . . let me jump into the shower first. Them niggas out there had me chasing they asses round the block for my cash tonight. I'll hit you off when I'm done, though," he said while moving toward the shower.

"Thick! Stop fuckin' playin' wit' me. Whenever you want me—sweaty, dirty, or not—I give it to you. Now I'm tellin' you right now to get the fuck over here."

"Yo, who the fuck you talkin' to?"

" 'Yo'?" she repeated. "Is that where she lives? In bamified-ass Baltimore?" Yvette asked, picking up on the "Yo" he used at the start of his sentence.

"Bitch, get the fuck out of my face and fix my food!" he said as he moved to the bathroom and got into the shower.

Frustrated, Yvette quickly picked up the phone to call her girl.

"Kenyetta, do me a favor?" she asked when her friend answered.

"No problem. What you need?" Kenyetta asked, willing to do whatever her girl wanted.

"Is Li'l C outside?"

"Yeah, he out here. Why?"

"Send him up here to get Thick's car keys. And I want you to run the overhaul on his ass for me."

Kenyetta knew exactly what the "overhaul" meant. It meant running through that nigga's truck, until she found any signs of him being with another bitch.

"I'm sending him up now," Kenyetta said, hanging up.

Five minutes later, with Thick still in the shower, Li'l C came upstairs.

Before she opened the door, she already had the money for him. Li'l C was young, but he wasn't stupid. He didn't do anything unless it was something in it for him. Although he had no idea of why he was giving Thick's car keys to Kenyetta, he did know that something was definitely up.

Handing him a crisp fifty-dollar bill, and reminding him to keep his mouth closed, she sent Li'l C back downstairs to complete her mission.

Ten minutes later, Thick got out of the shower, wrapped in a towel, and walked into their room to get dressed.

Black bastard! she thought. *Yeah, I got your ass now.*

Fifteen minutes later, Li'l C returned with the car keys. As he was handing them to Yvette, Thick walked out of the room and toward the door.

"What's up, li'l nigga? Where your father at?"

"I don't know, young!" he responded in that same arrogant tone.

"Word? Well, look, did your father give you them Jordans I picked up for you?"

"Yeah, thanks, man! Them joints is tight!"

"No problem, li'l nigga. What you doin' up here, anyway?" he asked casually.

Yvette, meanwhile, was scared to death. If Thick found out she sent somebody on a rampage through his truck, he would fuck her up. It never dawned on her that he might catch Li'l C bringing back the keys. She was dead set on her mission, and that was the bottom line. But she smiled as she found out that Li'l C had learned to lie already, like most men eventually do after they come out of Pampers.

"I came up here for you, man! I saw your truck out front and wanted to know if you can give me fifty bucks!"

Thick began to laugh, because he was amused that Li'l C was already about gettin' money. He liked him and liked the way he had turned out.

"I ain't got fifty, li'l nigga, but you can keep this hundred."

"That's what's up, Uncle Thick!" he said as he grabbed the cash and ran out the door.

That was smooth, Yvette thought, smiling with relief. *That boy made a hundred fifty dollars in less than twenty minutes.*

When her phone rang, she excused herself from Thick to answer it.

"If it's Carissa and them, tell them you tendin' to your nigga and can't be shootin' the shit wit' them all night. Y'all can talk later," he said sarcastically.

"Whatever, Thick!" Yvette shot back as she moved to the bedroom to take the call privately.

"Bitch, you heard me, right?"

"Yeah, Thick," she said, partially defeated.

"Make it quick!" he stated.

When he was done with his demands, she turned her attention back to the call.

"So what's up?" she whispered, anxious to see what Kenyetta had found.

"He ain't have no condoms or nothing like that."

Disappointment washed over Yvette. "Oh."

"But I did find something else, Yvette."

"What is it?" she asked as her heart rate sped up.

"His T-shirt was in the backseat, balled up. When I opened it, I saw some shit on it that looked like nut or somethin'."

"What?"

"Yeah, girl. Nut. Big T is definitely steppin' out on you."

Yvette had heard enough. She knew what kind of man she had, and she knew it was nut. He had taken his shirt off plenty of times when they were together sexually in the car and he always used it to wipe himself off. What hurt the most was that he had sex in a truck that was in her name. Thick didn't have credit and couldn't even get an apartment in his own name if he wanted. This was an extreme violation.

"Thanks, Kenyetta."

"You need anything?" she asked in a concerned tone. "Wanna get some drinks at my place?"

"Naw . . . I'll talk to you later." When she ended the call, she stared at him, unnoticed. It angered her that he was all posted up as if nothing had happened.

Always a soldier, she went about her day and cooked his meal. She wanted to say something but didn't.

Number one, he would fuck her up for violating his privacy; and number two, he'd be mad at Kenyetta for going into his truck.

She sucked it up, and then decided to follow him the next time he wanted to take one of his weekend trips. As tough as she was, the only thing that scared her was losing him. But something told her that she already had.

Chapter 13
Like Ballas Do
January, Friday, 9:30 P.M.

The Emerald City Squad

In a hotel conference room tucked away in downtown D.C., members of the Emerald City Squad were dressed in all black. Outside of their distinguishing facial features, all that could be seen in the room were platinum-and-diamond chains and diamond-emblazoned watches. The squad was coming up quickly; and at this point in the game, they could do anything they wanted financially.

The Emerald City Squad didn't cut corners when it came to their meetings. They believed that a man could do his best thinking when in the company of beautiful women, bomb weed, good drinks, and good food. So for entertainment they hired strippers from the former Club 55 and had every color—from dark chocolate to

French vanilla—to please their eyes. Fat breasts, small waists, and round asses aroused their minds, and their bodies. In the dimly lit room, four strippers, who were wearing nothing but black thongs and black stilettos with steel heels, were entertaining them while they held their monthly meeting.

Several issues needed to be addressed regarding Emerald City and their surrounding shops. Although not originally intended, the Emerald City Squad was quickly beginning to reign as the most vicious crew in D.C. Niggas knew from all around that if they messed with one of the shops EC ran, they would have to deal with the entire crew instead of just one of them.

"So what up wit' this Derrick thing? I hear that nigga's causing problems around Emerald City," Dyson said.

"What you mean, what's up wit' him? That nigga gettin' paper, so we all gettin' paper," Thick said, sipping Hennessy and Coke, while rubbing his hand up the thigh of one of the baddest strippers in Washington, D.C.

"That nigga may be getting paper for now," said Cameron, who was already tired of the shit Derrick was giving his fiancée, "but if he can't respect the girls, he gonna have to get paper somewhere else!"

Thick pushed the stripper to the side. "Oh, so you makin' the rules now?"

"I'm not makin' the rules, man, but I am

making sure that this issue gets some real fuckin' attention. Mercedes ain't blowin' *you* up every time this nigga feel like he don't wanna follow the rules—she blowin' me up! Now, we all know that Mercedes is in charge of collection. Since she gotta deal wit' this dude all the time, we need to put his ass in check!" he said, sipping Belvedere from his cup.

The meetings used to be run by Dex. After he was murdered, the squad decided to keep them going, with a new person running it each month. That person would be in charge of the strippers, food, and the location. They never held their meetings in the same location, leaving nothing to chance. They knew that the more predictable they appeared, the more they increased their chances of being caught slippin'. And with the heat they brought around the hood, they had made plenty of enemies.

Lavelle yelled, "Okay, calm down, everybody! We need to weigh everything before we make a decision about Derrick." He took a draw of his weed. "What exactly are the girls sayin' he's doin', Cam?"

"You know how women are—"

Before Cameron could finish speaking, Thick interrupted him. "Yeah, I know how they are. And that's what the fuck I'm talkin' about. Anytime you got bitches runnin' shit, niggas is gonna be mad emotional. It's natural. Shit, I don't want to hear half of the shit Zakayla be givin' me. It's in a man's nature to give a bitch orders, not take orders from 'em. Derrick just probably used to us runnin' shit—that's all."

Cameron added, "Well, shit has changed, Thick! The girls are holdin' down that operation for us."

"Ain't nothing changed, man. They still moody bitches. I'm sure if you talked to Derrick, he'd have something else to say about it. We shouldn't be comin' down on him on bullshit. That nigga's station stays pumpin'! Everybody gotta give."

"Yeah, but if we think like that, all we doin' is givin' niggas a free pass to fuck wit' them, which is fuckin' wit' our money," Lavelle insisted. "We got to keep niggas in check. Fuckin' wit' the girls should have the same repercussions as fuckin' wit' us would. *No fuckin' exceptions!*"

The squad fell silent. They knew what Lavelle was saying was right. Lavelle broke through the darkness in the dimly lit room by pulling from his weed. The smoke rising from it appeared to slice the silence.

"He's right," Thick said, although he hated to be made a fool of over something that now seemed so obvious. Allowing niggas to disrespect the girls—just because they were girls—could fuck wit' their business. He realized more than ever that no type of disrespect could be tolerated, simply because a nigga was salty. "I'll talk to Derrick."

"Naw, man, I think I should do it. You already

held the meeting with Doctanian's crew. Lettin' you go again would seem like you're the only one they need to be worried about," Dyson said as he sipped on his drink and pulled a stripper on his lap. "I'll go, instead."

Although Kenyetta had accused Dyson of cheating, he still wasn't the worst one out of the crew. He'd only fuck a girl to relieve stress. But Thick, on the other hand, had taken things to another level. Behind his back they all talked about how he was dirty for making Zakayla wifey instead of the woman who had helped build their organization. It wasn't the fucking or the cheating that made them upset. No, it was the fact that by doing Yvette greasy, he was shitting where he slept. The entire operation was on the line.

"Cool," Thick responded, angry that they had peeped a glimpse of the plan he had to take over Emerald City. "You can talk to him. But I think we should all be there—"

Cameron interrupted. "I don't. He hates confrontation, so I think Dyson should go alone. Derrick ain't doin' nothing stupid. He'll be a'ight."

With a simple nod of their heads, they reluctantly reached an agreement.

"All right. Let's move to the next issue. I think we should meet with the ladies more than we have been," Dyson added.

Thick spoke first, allowing the liquor and

weed to influence his thinking. "Man, you ain't 'bout to control my dick."

"What the fuck you talkin' about, T? Ain't nobody talkin' about your dick. What this nigga talking about?" Dyson laughed as he looked toward his friends and they began to laugh.

This display of entertainment at Thick's expense angered and embarrassed him.

"Well, what you talkin' 'bout then, nigga? Damn! What you really sayin'?"

"I'm sayin' that we should hold meetings with the girls each month. And instead of them givin' us bits and pieces of the status of Emerald City, they can give us everything all at once," Dyson continued.

"I agree. Running Emerald City ain't no joke, and for real they holdin' that shit down better than we did." Lavelle laughed. "We should help them out a little more by showing we got their backs."

"Okay. We'll meet with them before we have our meetings each month. That way, if there's an issue with them, we can bring it to the table and discuss how we want to handle it," Dyson concluded.

Thick was growing irritated that he wasn't coming up with any good ideas. "Is there anything else?" he grumbled. "I'm ready to get my dick sucked by one of these bitches."

"Yeah. Hold fast on that shit. One more thing," Dyson said as he gulped down his drink. "Are there any plans to get the girls out of Emerald City? I think livin' over there is fuckin' wit' them. And we all can agree that it's been about time."

This was the first time the question ever came up in a meeting. Individually they gave the women they claimed to love their own answers on the topic. But here in front of each other, they were forced to admit what was really on their minds.

"Why is this even bein' brought up?" Thick's voice boomed. "It ain't the right time for them to leave, and we know that shit! We need to continue to feed them bullshit, until we can trust somebody enough to run the control station. There's too much money pouring into Emerald City now to change shit up. One wrong move can fuck up everything. So what you bringin' up right now is bullshit." He continued in an audacious attempt to break down an issue that the rest of them felt was serious.

Thick pissing on Dyson's question made Cameron mad. "Look. I plan on marrying Mercedes. I got my li'l man and my girls over there too. Now, I'm not afraid of the hood, but my girl ain't happy there no more. It's easy for us to say that shit should be cool, because most of us ain't there but two or three days out of the week. But they livin' over there twenty-four–seven. That shit ain't right, I'm tellin' y'all now."

"I'm wit' Cameron. My two li'l girls are over there, man. This ain't gonna fly for long. They can run shit off EC the same way we do," Lavelle added.

Thick stood up and walked around the table. His sudden movement caused the strippers to scatter. "What I want to know is who the fuck are we *really* loyal to? We have a fuckin' business to run. It ain't like we took them out of suburbia and moved them into the projects. They were born, raised, and bred in them muthafuckas! I say this issue shouldn't even be addressed, until we pump enough fear in that muthafucka that niggas won't even attempt to fuck wit' us. Until then, this shit is dead." Without waiting for a response, he sat back down and picked up his cup.

From the outside, the Emerald City Squad appeared to be falling apart. But in some of their minds, this tension could make them closer if they came through it. Still, Cameron and Lavelle felt it was easy for Thick to trample all over the issue, because he wasn't feeling Yvette anymore. But for them it was hard, because they had vowed to be true to the ones they were in love with.

On the other hand, they swore loyalty to the crew. But sooner or later, something or somebody was going to have to give.

Chapter 14

Too Much Mouth

January, Tuesday, 9:00 A.M.

Derrick

Derrick was deep into his main girl's pussy.

Her pussy wasn't as tight as he liked it to be, but she knew how to work her muscles so well that it really didn't matter. Even though she was his main girl, it was only because he didn't spend time with anybody else. He was too busy. As lieutenant of the Emerald City's Unit C Squad, his real time was spent banking money, and watching over his soldiers.

After busting all of his nut on Shannon's face, he made her get up and grab him a warm washcloth from the bathroom. He couldn't stand lying in the smell of sex for too long. But he didn't feel like moving either. Shannon returned with the wet washcloth and began gently wiping his dick down. When she was done with him, she wiped her mouth, hopped onto the bed next to him, and began tracing the outline of his muscles with her index finger.

"So what you doin' today? Can you take me to the movies or somethin'?"

"What I tell you 'bout tryin' to make plans wit' me during the week?"

She stared at him, trying to remember.

"Don't," he reminded her.

She jumped up and searched the cold floor for her panties. "Well, why not? It seems like all we do is fuck!"

"What's the problem?" He slid to the floor to do his routine of one hundred sit-ups and one hundred push-ups. "Besides, you knew from the jump that's all I could give you."

"Please! Save that bullshit! The moment I start feelin' somebody else, you get an attitude!"

He stopped in mid–sit-up. "Is that what you think?" He let out a disgusted sound. "Because I don't give a fuck who you deal wit', just as long as it ain't nobody from round here."

She stood over him and put her foot on his chest. "Well, I guess you wouldn't be worried. Seein' as though you still checking behind a woman you can never have."

He pushed her foot off. "That's your problem. You running your mouth 'bout shit you don't know 'bout. If your mouth wasn't so quick, maybe I could take you a little more seriously. But no woman on my arm can have a mouth like yours."

"Are you sure about that, Derrick? I mean, you tell me all the time about how Mercedes be kickin' shit to you, yet you still like her." She walked away, searching for her bra and clothes.

Shannon's words made him angry. Not because they were lies, but because he didn't know what he was feeling. He hated the idea of somebody else knowing something he didn't. As far as he knew, Mercedes was just a pretty face; and like most women, she had a mouth. He hated how she bossed him around or tried to play him in front of his crew when their money was to be collected. So while part of him was attracted to her, an equal part of him hated her guts.

He wiped his face with the towel on the dresser and stood up. "Look, I gotta go out there and get my money. So put your shit on and get out."

"Whatever, nigga, I'm leavin', anyway! You are so fuckin' sorry. You know if Cameron finds out you're jocking for his girl, you just might show up missing."

Shannon's mouth set him off. He rushed her and pushed her against the wall with his hand around her neck. Shannon's eyes were so big that he thought they might pop out of her head. She clawed at his arms while trying to secure her next breath.

"What you got to say now, bitch?"

Shannon's face began to turn red.

"Like I said, your mouth is the main reason I will never fuck with you on a serious tip. Now get your shit and get the fuck outta here!"

When he released her, she brushed her soft wavy hair out of her face and headed to the bathroom to put on the rest of her clothes. She couldn't wrap her mind around why she even continued to fuck with him. But when she put on her one-carat-diamond earrings and diamond tennis bracelet, she was quickly reminded. Derrick spent money on her, and good money at that. He wasn't buying a relationship; he was buying her time. As long as he gave her money, he expected her to be accessible to him anytime he wanted her, with no questions asked. But lately she was trying to be more like a wife, instead of the paid prostitute she really was.

In the kitchen Derrick drank some orange juice and ate an apple. His body was his temple and he didn't put anything in it, unless it was pure. No fast food or processed goods went into his body. Although he smoked weed, he'd combat anything somebody said about that by saying it was grown naturally. He was a powerhouse inside and out. Books by Malcolm X, Huey Newton, and other black activists filled the bookshelf on the wall. He was by far more different on the inside than most people knew. But he preferred it that way—the less they knew about him, the better.

When Shannon finished dressing, Derrick approached her before she left out the door. She hoped that he felt bad for how he treated her and was going to apologize. She placed it out of her mind after realizing that Derrick apologizing was as far-fetched as him making her his girl.

"Shannon . . . next time you come around here, just tell them bitches what they need to know. Don't bullshit them when you come through them gates. Them girls ain't playin'. It's business."

Trying to bite her tongue, while not trying to piss him off, was becoming harder for her to do. Still, she realized she'd gain nothing by making him more upset than he already was.

"I will. . . . But just so you know, Carissa got mad at me and Sharonda because we knew Lavelle. She acted like it was a crime to know him or something."

He took one step closer to her. "What you talkin' 'bout girl?"

"Well, you know he fuckin' Sharonda, right? Well . . . we mentioned we knew him, just tryin' to see where her head was at, and she got all bent out of shape." The light from his kitchen bounced off the earrings and the honey brown fur coat that she wore, courtesy of his money.

"Why the fuck would y'all do that bamma shit?" he yelled.

She shrugged her shoulders. "I don't know. She was actin' all high and mighty, and we thought it'd be funny to put her back in her place. We was just fuckin' with her. It wasn't that serious. After we finished playin' her, we told her what she needed to know."

"Shannon, get the fuck out! And don't call me, I'll call you." He opened the door and slammed it behind her.

Bitches! he thought. He didn't understand why she would have Sharonda in the car in the first place. Let alone hint around to her fucking Lavelle. *I swear that bitch gonna make me knock her ass out!*

He decided not to give any more thought to it because the damage had been done and there wasn't anything he could do to change it. He just jumped into the shower, and prepared himself for work.

"Walk wit' me for a sec, man," Dyson said as he pulled up on Derrick working in the yard.

"What about my soldiers? You know a lot of shit been goin' on around here."

"I know, man. Put one of your best on lookout and meet me around back, near the community center."

Fifteen minutes later, Derrick did what he

was told. Eager to find out what was up, he hustled around the back of Unit C to the community center. Noticing Dyson was sitting in his white BMW 750i, Derrick jumped into the passenger seat and locked the door. Once in, Dyson handed him a blunt and Derrick pulled on it.

He laughed as he took another pull before passing it. "So what up, man? I know you ain't come here to pass the bob wit' me."

Dyson nodded in agreement as he pulled on the weed inside the cherry-tasting blunt paper. "Naw, I didn't. But it's a hell of an icebreaker, ain't it? This shit comes from my Jamaican connect, and it moves faster than I can get it in."

"For real? Well, why we ain't got none of this over here?" Derrick asked.

"Because Dreyfus supplies everything for EC, man. And he wouldn't appreciate nothing but his product movin' over here. Well, look, nigga, I ain't out here to beat around the bush. I just figured I'd hit you off wit' a little bit of ganja before I tell you what I need to tell you."

"And what's that?"

"You need to stop fuckin' wit' Mercedes and them." He reached under his seat and put his .38 in his lap, with the barrel facing Derrick.

Derrick instantly got heated. "So it's like that? You come out here and pull your weapon on me?"

"Naw, muthafucka! What it's like is that you gotta stop fuckin' wit' 'em. If you know the money's due, or they need you on somethin' else, you best be handlin' it," Dyson barked.

Derrick tried to calm down. "So y'all listen to them, without even hearing me out. This some bullshit, young."

"Whatever, nigga. You knew we'd be out here sooner or later. We let you fuck with them too long. Now, I know you got a problem with answering to females, but your problem stops here. You take orders from them, the same way you did from us. *Usted comprende?*"

Derrick was angry. He felt like reaching into his jeans and stuffing his 9mm into the same mouth that Dyson had just used to pull on that blunt. But working in Emerald City was good money, and this type of shit came with the territory.

So instead of shooting off, he listened.

"Now, this shit here requires teamwork. Me and the niggas know you handlin' your soldiers. But we won't have a problem cutting you off, if you can't get with the program. The *full* program."

"I can get wit' it. But I don't agree with how this is goin' down."

"And why you say that?" Dyson handed him the blunt and Derrick refused.

"I think y'all got shit messed up. I ain't got no problem answering to anybody that's filling my pockets. You can believe that! What I have a problem wit' is somebody tryin' to carry me in front of my soldiers. Do you know they had one of my workers come and get me while we were on the grind, because Critter say I ain't give him a tester? What kind of bullshit is that?"

"Well, was it true?" Dyson asked, pulling on the last of his weed before putting it out.

"I can't remember, man." Derrick lied, knowing full well he couldn't stand Critter. "But even if it was true, that's some bullshit to be callin' somebody up on, don't you think?"

"Not necessarily. Critter may be a fiend, but he's loyal to Emerald City. That's why we keep him around, and the girls realize that. Putting him on gives us an edge on some of these other projects around the way. That nigga know everybody, even the top officials from when he was in office."

"What office?" Derrick asked.

"Government office. Critter use to be a public official in D.C. Everybody knows that shit. Although he fell off like most muthafuckas do in this game, some of his old friends keep in contact, just so they can be put on to our dope. Plus it was Critter who told us that Charles and them tried to get Carissa. If it wasn't for him, we would've never known who those muthafuckas was."

So it was Critter's ass who told them, Derrick thought. *I wonder how he found out. It don't matter. They deserved to die for biting the hand that feeds them.*

125

Derrick took a deep breath and tried to blow out some tension. "It's like this, Dyson. Tell 'em to ease off of me and I'll ease off of them. I can't run my camp if my soldiers think I'm soft."

"Cool. I'll tell 'em to stop sweatin' you 'bout bullshit, but you gotta do your part too."

When they finished, Derrick went back to work, but with Mercedes on his mind. As far as he was concerned, it was just a matter of time before they dealt with each other.

Chapter 15

Busted

January, Wednesday, 10:37 P.M.

Yvette

I finally broke down and told my friends everything that was goin' on between Thick and me.

What messed me up was that most of them already seemed to know he was steppin' out on me. They acted like it wasn't even a surprise. Outside of having Kenyetta go check his truck, I hadn't told anybody we were having problems.

We were doing a stakeout and I had already seen enough to run up on him. But knowing Thick, I realized he'd turn it around into something else, unless I had proof. So with Mercedes' digital camera, we were trying to get some good pictures of him taking her to Charlie Palmer Steak in D.C. and to the Shakespeare Theatre Company.

Yeah, he was really pulling out the stops for this bitch. But nothing hurt worse than seeing who he was dealing with. It was the same girl from the day of the funeral and from Tiffany. I didn't tell my friends, but I wondered if the rock she had on her finger was an engagement ring. Please, God, don't let it be. I wanted to believe that he wouldn't be crazy enough to propose to someone else over me; but right now, I wasn't sure of anything.

"They comin' out of the theater right now!" Kenyetta yelled from the backseat of the Grand Prix we rented. I sat next to her slumped down in my seat. I didn't want Thick to see me.

But for real, he was *still* slippin'. Recognizable car or not, he should've known that somebody had been following him for so long.

But there he was, just as sure as it was night, coming out of the theater, wearing the dark gray slacks and jacket that I paid for. He looked like a million bucks when he cleaned up; and with his body and build, I knew she was losing her mind.

"Did he just kiss her?" Mercedes asked as she took pictures of them in the truck. She was in the front with Carissa.

"It looked like it," Carissa said. "Thick has lost his muthafuckin' mind. I say we run up on him right now, before they pull off. Fuck da bullshit."

"I'm wit' Carissa, Yvette," Kenyetta added, looking at me for approval. "We seen enough. Let's handle this shit now."

They were right, but I didn't want to do it right here. I needed to find out where she lived and where he'd been laying his head every night. So for forty-five minutes, we followed them to her apartment in Baltimore. The moment I saw him leaned up against his truck with her in front of him, kissing on him, I decided to jump out.

My heart dropped as the man I would have done anything for violated me. Here I was, his flunky, running an operation that he should've taken care of; and this was how he repaid me— by breaking my fucking heart.

We all got out of the car, but they couldn't keep the pace I was givin'. With his arms wrapped around her, and his tongue in her mouth, I snuck up on him from the side of his big-ass truck and said, "Is it that good to you? That you would risk everything we have together?"

He stopped and on instinct pushed her away. She immediately backed up, sensing what I was gettin' ready to give. And as mad as I was, I knew she wasn't ready for it either.

"What you doin' here, Yvette? Who watchin' EC?" he yelled, trying to flip the shit and put it back on me.

"Fuck you, Thick! Is this where you've been going? Is this where you've been spending your time? With this bitch?"

I was loud, and I didn't care. I wanted to break up the peaceful serenity in the place where

129

she lived. Why should she live like a queen and my living conditions be fucked up? Here I was, living with fiends and criminals, and this bitch was over here in B-More, living like a princess.

"Who you callin' a bitch?" she snapped.

I ignored her, because I was focused on his bitch ass now, and my girls were already on the job.

"I'm tellin' you right now, if you want your ass whipped, make anotha muthafuckin' move!" Carissa said, with her hand in her purse.

Yeah, bitch! I thought. *This is how we do it! South side–style, baby!*

Thick's tramp was so shook that she didn't move.

"Answer the question, Thick! Is it worth it? I see you livin' it up out here, and got me living in trash. Why, Thick? Why you doin' this to me?"

"You livin' in trash? Are you serious? You wouldn't be living in trash if you'd clean your fuckin' house, you nasty bitch! Half of the time I ain't home because it's too muthafuckin' dirty! I'm tired of that shit, Yvette!"

The embarrassment I felt overwhelmed me.

I felt like I did the best I could do. He wanted me outside fourteen hours a day, and he wanted me to be his wife, mother, and friend. I didn't have time to clean my house, and I barely had time for myself.

"So now you tryin' to play me in front of your bitch and my friends? If you had a problem wit' somethin', why you ain't tell me, Thick? You are dead wrong right now, and you're actin' like I'm the one to blame. Why, baby? Don't you love me?"

He was silent, and I was hurt. Here we were, standing outside in front of the friends I considered family, and the love of my life acted like he could care less about me. The only comfort I had right now were my girls. I knew all I had to do was say the word, and they'd stomp his pretty girlfriend out. How much would he like her then?

"Let me ask you somethin', Thick, and be real wit' me. Are you gonna marry this bitch?" I asked him, but I was not really prepared for the answer. "I see the ring on her finger, but since you ain't bother to put one on mine, I wanna know."

The bitch called from the sideline, "Tell her the truth, Thick. Let's get this over with."

"Listen, bitch! Mind your muthafuckin' business before I kick your fuckin' ass!" I yelled. I was tired of her mouth. I hadn't addressed her yet, because I believed in dealing with the man. But since she insisted to get in the business, she was getting ready to see how I beat bitches down on the block.

"Naw, you ain't doin' that," Thick said, taking up for her. "You ain't gonna fuckin' touch her."

"And why not? She's stealin' my man *and* talkin' shit," I told him as tears rolled down my face.

"You ain't doin' that because she's carrying

131

my baby. Now, I'm sorry you found out like this, but tonight I'm celebrating. She givin' me somethin' you never could. A son."

For a few seconds there was nothing but complete silence. I never realized that Baltimore had peaceful places like this. All I could hear were the crickets trying to be heard above the low hum of passing cars. My world was ending. Everything that I fought for, and everything that I believed in, was vanishing. I didn't understand why.

"Ugghh, Thick! I didn't even know you were grimy like that!" Mercedes said. "This don't make no damn sense!"

"This between us!" he yelled. "So step the fuck off."

His new girlfriend quickly moved to his side as he put his arm around her to comfort her.

He used to do that to me. What changed? What fucking changed! I loved him with all my heart, and I felt like that wasn't good enough.

My eyes filled with tears blurring my vision. He didn't even bother to console me. He just looked at me as if I was another issue he had to deal with before moving on with his life. The anger I had before diminished. I decided that I had one chance to fight for my man. One last chance. On my knees, outside in front of my friends and the bitch who had stolen my man's heart, I begged.

"Baby . . . please don't do this to me," I said as

I grabbed his leg. "Please don't leave me like this. I'll be a better woman to you, I swear. On my life I promise to be everything you need."

His girlfriend, huffing and puffing, didn't bother me. I knew I was disgracing myself, but I would've felt worse if I didn't at least try.

"You gotta give me a chance, baby. I'll lose weight, clean my house better—anything you want, I will do. I'm nothing without you, Thick. Everything I do don't mean shit, unless I have you in my life. Baby, please. I'm the one. I'm the one you trust, baby. I'm the one that would lay down my life for you. Don't walk out on me, Thick."

I could hear my friends crying behind me. Kenyetta had already walked to the car, because it was too much for her. But I felt that nobody understood more than they did why I was doing what I was doing. I knew those tears were filled with sorrow for me, and the realization that this could have been them right now. And I'd put my life on it: they'd be doing the same thing too.

But my pleas landed on deaf ears. He kicked me off his leg like I was a crackhead trying to get a rock. My friends rushed by my side and helped me up. And it's a good thing they did, because my legs couldn't move. All I could think about was what I could've possibly done to deserve this.

"It's over, Yvette. You and me are business

partners, but this right here is my future wife. Now, I'm sorry it gotta go down like this. I really am. But I'm not in love with you no more. I didn't know it was gonna turn out like this, but what we had ends here."

"I'm glad you laughing, bitch! Cuz he gonna do the same thing to you too!" Mercedes yelled.

"Fuck you, Mercedes!" he yelled.

"*No*, fuck *you*, you sorry-ass muthafucka!" she shot back.

His new girl smiled at me as she faded in the dark with my life. He held her hand and moved toward the apartment building. He stopped short and turned around.

My heart skipped as I thought he was gonna tell me he made a mistake. That maybe we could work on us, after all. But what he said next only proved more that he was through with me.

"I hope this don't affect our business relationship. You the hardest-working nigga I know. I'll check you later," he said as he walked off into the night.

Heartbroken and humiliated, I sat in the backseat as my friends drove me home. I wondered to myself how I was ever gonna make it . . . *alone*.

Chapter 16

Wishing Things Were the Way They Used to Be

January, Wednesday, 6:37 P.M.

Mercedes

It had been three weeks since Thick and Yvette split.

My girl had been taking it bad. She wasn't on post anymore, and Emerald City was quickly going down with her. Cameron and the others made their presence known; but with them still holding down the other shops outside of EC, they weren't around as much. Several of our runners had been robbed, and we were startin' to wonder if they weren't a part of everything that was going on.

"Carissa, one of Harold's soldiers is missin' in

action. I think we should go see what's up wit'
'em," I told her as I ended the call with Harold
and placed the phone under my chair.

"Damn! I hope he ain't tryin' to do us
greasy," Carissa said while zipping her Baby Phat
waist-length coat.

"I'll be glad when Yvette get it together. We
need her out here!" Kenyetta said.

"You ain't lyin'. How long has he been missin'
in action?" Carissa asked.

"A week and a half. The thing is this, you
know Harold's squad has been hit more than
once over the past week. I'm starting to think
it's an inside job."

"Well, who slackin'?" Carissa asked, sensing
how serious things were.

"It's Key. They probably smokin' up our shit
right now."

It's easy to spot which soldiers respect their
captains when the going gets rough. Nobody on
Doctanian's, Derrick's, Bruce's and Jones's
teams got out of line. Just because we were having issues among ourselves didn't mean it was
time for everybody else to fall apart. See, Doctanian and them were respected captains and
had their soldiers in check, with the exception
of one of them who attempted to get away. And
because of it, nobody tried them as much as
they did Harold's and Ed's teams. We didn't
have any problem from any other squad, outside of those two.

"Okay. Let's go over to Unit B and see what's up," Carissa responded.

"I'm right behind you."

The hallway was dark; the lighting was poor; and thanks to the leak at the other end of the corridor, it smelled musty. Before stepping off the elevator, we scanned the floor. We wanted to make sure another situation didn't happen to us, like the one that had happened to Carissa.

We quickly moved down the hall toward the apartment. Unfortunately, we couldn't see the apartment due to the bend in the hallway. We arrived at the door and heard voices coming from inside. I placed my hand on my heat and Carissa did the same. We never went anywhere without our fire; and although we had them, we never had to use them. However, if Yvette didn't come back to work, I knew it would be just a matter of time before that changed.

We knocked firmly on the door three times. There was no answer, but the chatter on the inside stopped.

Before we could knock again, the door flew open. The person who opened it stepped behind it, giving us a clear view of the inside. Before going in, I stuck my head around the corner and saw it was Key's older brother, Deuce.

"Come on in," he said, blowing out smoke.

"Is Key here?" Carissa asked before going any farther inside.

He nodded toward the living room. "Yeah, he ova there."

When we walked in, Carissa went before me, and I fell back a little. I didn't want anybody rushing us from behind, so I wanted to make sure we had all angles covered. I hated having my back turned in places I didn't know. There were six dudes in the dirty one-bedroom apartment. Two of them were sitting on a broken ottoman in front of the television, playing *NBA Live*. Two more were sitting on the couch. Deuce was standing up, while the other one was at the kitchen table, rolling weed.

"That's a nice ring, Mercedes," Deuce said. "You and Cameron must be stackin' mad money."

As hard as it was, I just ignored his dumb ass.

"Where's Key?" I asked, realizing he wasn't in sight or included in the six men I had counted when we stepped into the apartment.

One of the men sitting on the couch said, "He in the room. He'll be out in a second."

The smell of the apartment was sickening. The dingy walls and dirty carpet told the story of endless drinking and smoking sessions. There was a table filled with weed and the insides of Phillies Blunt papers covered it throughout. The couch looked like it used to be a cream color, but it was damn near black.

138

One minute later, Key appeared from a back room, visibly high.

"What up? What you need?" he asked as he joined his friends on the couch. "I know you ain't come over here to give me no pussy. I hear Lavelle and them bangin' y'all's backs out." He laughed with the others.

Carissa looked at me. With my hand on my piece, I made sure I kept my eyes on every one of them. My senses were so heightened that even in the dim lighting of the apartment, I could tell which one of them needed to shower and who was wearing Sean John jeans. I was willing to bust somebody's ass just for moving wrong.

"I need to know why you ain't been back to work. What's up wit' that? You ain't in here smokin' our shit, are you?" Carissa asked.

He laughed. "Smokin' *your* shit? Naw. I ain't smoke nothin' that belong to *you*."

"Okay. Well, give us your product and money and we'll be gone. And don't bother about comin' back on the block, you cut off!" I jumped in.

"What the fuck you talkin' 'bout? I don't ansa to yo ass! I ansa to your nigga!"

"Fuck you talkin' 'bout, Key? You answer to everybody, muthafucka! We put the cash in your hand every week. Now you know the muthafuckin' routine. Either ante up our money or product, or you *will* be dealt with," Carissa added.

From the way things were looking, she was passing out threats that I was sure we would have to follow through with.

With hate in his eyes, he stood up and moved toward Carissa. " 'Dealt with'? And just how do you plan on dealing wit' me? What you gonna do? Suck my dick?"

Carissa backed away from him and moved toward me, pushing both of us toward the front door. All of them stood up, and I could see that whatever was getting ready to happen was gonna be real bad. They outnumbered us; and although we had guns, there was no tellin' what they had on them.

I grabbed Carissa's arm as we scooted closer to the door. I knew that whatever happened at this point would have to be done by the EC Squad. I hated Yvette not being with us; because although she didn't say it, I knew she had at least two bodies on her gun.

With Carissa behind me, I snatched open the door and bolted toward the elevators. I could hear my heart beatin' in my ears. I couldn't wait to tell Cameron and the rest of them what had happened.

When I reached the elevator, I turned around. My heart sank to my stomach because Carissa wasn't behind me.

Without hesitation I ran back down the hall and started banging on the door with my gun in hand, demanding they open it. When the door flung open, I trained my gun on his gully ass. "Where the fuck is my girl, nigga?"

"Hold up. Hold up! W-what the f-fuck you doin', yo?" he stammered. "Your girl ain't here, man! Now put that shit down before somebody get hurt!"

"What the fuck you mean she ain't here?" I asked, desperately trying to stop the tears from forming in my eyes. I didn't want to remind them that I was a woman and afraid.

Without asking permission I pushed my way in and ran through all four rooms, including the kitchen and bathroom, but I still didn't see her. Excessive amounts of sweat caused my hair to cling to my forehead and my clothes to cling to my body. I felt light-headed; I knew in my heart that they had done something to my friend. There was no way in hell I was burying another friend!

"Where in the fuck is my friend?" I demanded, pressing my 9mm to one of their heads. I didn't care anymore. If they killed my friend, one of them was going with her.

"Listen, bitch! We let you run through here. If you ain't see her, that mean she ain't in here. Now get the fuck out!" the older man said as he pushed me toward the door and into the hall-way. When the door slammed behind me, I fell to my knees and banged on it harder, but they didn't open it.

Afraid that I had lost my friend, I ran to the

elevator to get help. I reached for my iPhone and my heart dropped. I had left it on the porch! Shit!

The first person I saw when I got off the elevator was Derrick. Seeing the look of terror on my face must've set him off, because he ran to my side to help me.

"What's wrong, shawty? Somebody fuckin' wit' you?"

Through tears and trying to catch my breath, I tried to tell him everything that had happened. The look on his face, although angry, comforted me. I could tell that he would find out what the fuck had happened—even if it meant taking somebody out.

We got back on the elevator, and then I took him to the door.

"This Key house! I just left outta here," he said as he knocked on the door.

Deuce saw him through the peephole and, without hesitation, opened it for him.

"Sorry, nigga. We thought you were that bitch!" he said. "Come on in, man."

Before they could close the door, I pushed my way in. Derrick knocked Deuce out with the back of his gun. I held my gun firmly in the direction of them muthafuckas because I was sure my friend was dead.

"What you doin', Joe?" He called him by the name most D.C. natives gave everyone. "Is this bitch lying to you too?" Key asked as he jumped up.

Derrick cocked his gun and cut the light on, revealing how truly dirty and nasty the apartment really was.

"I'ma ask you one time. If you don't tell me what I wanna hear, you gonna have four more holes in your face. Now, where the fuck is Carissa?"

"I'm telling you the truth! I don't know where that bitch at," Key said, clearly intimidated by Derrick's presence.

"So why the fuck are y'all huddled up on the sofa like some fuckin' bitches lookin' guilty?"

His comment caused me to look in that direction. When Carissa and I came to the apartment, they were all spread apart. Now all five of them were huddled on the couch like they were in love. That's when I saw my girl's hand behind one of the back pillows on the sofa. They were using their bodies to conceal the bump in the sofa, which was Carissa.

"Derrick!" I screamed. "She's behind the pillows on the sofa!"

"What?" He moved toward them.

"They're hiding her under the pillows of that nasty-ass couch!" I said as tears ran down my face.

All of them immediately looked shook. Derrick moved toward the couch, knocking one of them in the face with the gun. I knew right then they were some punks who were only willing to talk shit to women. But when a man approached them, they had their heart taken.

Throwing the pillows on the floor, Derrick lifted her limp body. I noticed the blood flowing from her head; I was instantly filled with rage. They probably snatched her back on the way out the door and covered her mouth. In one motion I cocked my gun and put two in Key's head. His friends scattered, trying desperately to avoid being next.

I was about to pull the trigger again, but Derrick grabbed me and told me to come on. I didn't care if war was about to be staged. They violated the rules in a major way.

"We can finish this later." Derrick's voice bought me back to reality as he cradled Carissa in his arms.

We ran down the hallway. I didn't take another breath until we were on the elevator, and I saw Carissa open her eyes.

Chapter 17

Finally

January, Friday, 9:15 P.M.

Zakayla

Zakayla was on cloud nine before she went to the doctor's office.

She had everything she wanted, including the man for whom she had fought so hard over the past two years to have. He had given her everything she ever wanted.

She wasn't remorseful at all about how Thick had treated Yvette. She believed all of the stories he had told her about how nasty Yvette was and how she constantly cheated on him. In Zakayla's mind Yvette and Thick would've broken up eventually. Zakayla truly believed that she was capable of treating him the way that he should've been treated, since Yvette clearly could not.

All of her happiness was squashed when the

doctor entered the cold exam room and pissed on her dreams.

"I'm sorry, Ms. Taylor, but you're not pregnant. Take this chart and accurately record your cycle so you can tell when you're ovulating. Don't give up."

"Are you sure? Maybe you should check it again," she begged, looking over the small chart.

"I'm positive, Ms. Taylor." He smiled, placing one hand on her shoulder. "But if you monitor your cycle more closely, your chances to conceive will be increased."

In her mind lying to Thick about being pregnant was the only way she could've convinced him to leave Yvette, and it worked.

"Girl, it's negative again," Zakayla told her friend Lacretia as she drove home and chatted on her phone.

"Well, you know what you have to do, right?" she asked.

"What?"

"Just keep fuckin' him!" She laughed. "You'll get pregnant, girl."

"I know, I know, but he thinks I'm three months pregnant now! The further along he thinks I am, the harder it's gonna be for me to pass another pregnancy off on this one. The times will be too messed up."

"I understand all that, but at least you'll be pregnant. Thick ain't thinkin' about when the baby is born. He just wants to have a baby! But I do wish you hadn't told him it was a boy. Men are so stupid! A woman would've known that it was too early to tell."

"You're right, but the damage is done. And I'm starting to think I can't have kids," she responded as she pulled into the parking lot of her apartment complex.

"You can have kids, girl. You're healthy. Don't even worry about that. Anyway, has he talked to his ex?"

"No . . . but he said she's been fuckin' up bigtime. He has her runnin' one of his shops in D.C., but she ain't been comin' to work lately. Ever since he dumped her for me, she's been falling apart."

"His ex-girlfriend sells drugs for him!" Lacretia yelled through the earpiece.

"Yes, girl. I told you she was a dumb bitch. I wish Thick *would* ask me to do some bullshit like that. I would cut his ass off so quick that he wouldn't know what happened."

"Well, maybe he was using her all along. Like you said, she didn't even clean her own apartment." Lacretia laughed. "I'm surprised he stayed that long."

"Right, girl!"

Deep in her heart, though, Zakayla knew Thick still cared about Yvette, and the possibility of Thick leaving her one day was a chance she was willing to take. Unlike Yvette, Zakayla didn't tell him she wasn't ready to have a baby. She paid close attention to everything he said, and she made sure she was everything that Yvette *wasn't*.

"Well, let me go. Thick wants me to cook this big-ass meal for him tonight. Girl, my man is so fucking greedy." She laughed. "Good thing that nigga is paid—otherwise, he'd eat us outta house and home."

"Well, call me back later."

"Okay. I will."

When she ended the call, she grabbed her purse and parked her silver Navigator, which Thick had purchased for her as a gift for being pregnant with his first baby. When she stepped out of the truck, she dropped her keys on the ground and bent down to pick them up.

She had her back turned when she was grabbed by her hair and dragged along the ground toward the nearby woods at the complex. Zakayla fought, desperately kicking and screaming the entire way.

"Shut the fuck up, bitch, before I slice your throat!" one of them yelled.

She did what they said, hoping it was just a robbery. "Take everything." She was crying. "You can take my truck, my purse, everything."

"Don't worry. We will be taking exactly what we came for."

She was able to see that there were four of them, but their faces were covered in black ski masks. Repeatedly they kicked her in her face and stomach. The pain took over Zakayla's entire body as she begged them to stop. Judging by how hard they were kicking her, she could tell that they wanted her dead.

When she thought it couldn't get any worse, one of them slid off her rings, including the engagement ring that Thick had just purchased for her. Her mind slipped back and forth, in and out of consciousness.

"This is what happens when you fuck wit' a man that don't belong to you!" a female voice said. Although she was facedown in the dirt, with the grass partially covering her face, and the blood dripping in her eyes, she could tell by the curves in their bodies that they were all women.

When she saw three of them running toward the light, a few feet over from where they took her, she thought she might survive. That's when the fourth person hit her in the head with a bat. She was knocked unconscious.

When Zakayla came to, she was in a hospital room, with flowers and cards surrounding her. When she tried to lift her head, she couldn't move it. Moving her eyes down as far as she could, she saw the tissue from the bandages on her face.

She looked as far as she could to the left, where she saw Thick talking to Cameron,

Dyson, and Lavelle. She smiled a little, seeing that her man was right at her side.

When Thick saw her eyes open, they all ran to her side.

He held one of the only parts of her body not covered in a cast. "You need anything?"

"Some ice," she said, barely above a whisper. "What happened? What's wrong with me?"

"I'll let the doctor tell you baby," he said as he moved toward the door.

When the doctor entered the room, he asked if he could be left alone with her for a little while. When everybody was gone, Zakayla addressed him. Terror had consumed her.

"What's wrong with me?" She knew that something definitely happened because of her being jumped.

"Zakayla," the doctor started, his tone even but comforting. "I'm Dr. Polanski, and you're at Howard County General Hospital Center. It's remarkable that you survived." He smiled. "But you've suffered an extensive amount of damage to your spine. And there's a real possibility that you'll never be able to walk again."

"No. No," she said as tears fell, soaking the bandages on her face.

The look on the doctor's face made matters worse. She could tell that he was far from finished telling her about everything she needed to know.

"What else?" she asked, unsure if she would be able to take it.

"Well, Ms. Taylor, we've brought in the best reconstructive surgeons around."

"For what?" she cried out. Then her voice faded away as soon as it left her body.

"For your face, Ms. Taylor, for your face. It appears that whoever has done this to you took a blade and sliced your face over fifty times."

Zakayla felt weak; the doctor appeared to be moving farther and farther away from her. She felt like she was moving into darkness; she decided to let it consume her.

The more she tried to talk, the more it appeared to be in vain.

Within minutes she was unconscious.

Chapter 18

I'm Trying

January, Saturday, 12:18 P.M.

Yvette

Today was the first day I felt like going on.

I never realized how much Thick meant to me, until he was gone. I unplugged my phone weeks ago because I couldn't bear to see the calls from everyone but him. If he wasn't calling me, I didn't feel like talking.

The first thing I did was move everything out of my apartment and into the basement. The only things I had left were my mattress and TVs. I didn't want anything in my place that reminded me of Thick or the life I had with him. I decided that today I was going to get into my car, buy me some new furniture, and start all over. And because I hadn't eaten in weeks, I'd lost a lot of weight. So I'd have to buy some new clothes. I didn't realize how much weight I had lost until I tried to slide into a pair of old jeans, and they fell off.

When I plugged in my phone, I was afraid to check my messages. I'd been ignoring calls from everybody since Thick dumped me. People got tired of me ignoring their calls and started knockin' on my door, but I didn't open it. All I wanted was to be alone.

For the first week after the breakup, I had done nothin' but cry. And when I couldn't cry anymore, I thought about killin' myself. By the third week, however, I thought about killin' him. I put that idea out of my mind, though, because I loved him too much. I wanted to talk to my friends, but I put that out of my mind too. I was too embarrassed, because I knew they knew how long I had played his fool.

I decided to check my voice mails. And just as I had thought, my mailbox was full. The first message I heard was from Cameron, then Lavelle, and then Dyson. I erased them all. I'm sure they were wondering why I wasn't takin' care of my responsibilities with Emerald City, but I knew they understood too. And because I wasn't sure how I was gonna handle things yet, I didn't want to listen to their messages. The next voice I heard made me sad all over again, but I listened, anyway.

"What's up, Yvette? It's Thick. Now, I know we got problems, ma, but this ain't got shit to do with our business with Emerald City. I need you to be strong and handle this shit, like I know you can. I still love you. One."

He still loves me? Yeah, right! Fuck him. I ain't doin' shit else for him. He lost his flunky! If I do decide to go back on the block, it'll be for my girls and not him, I thought as I erased through the next few messages from my mom and my friends. I was good, until I heard the last one from Mercedes, crying.

"Yvette . . . please pick up! It's Mercedes! Girl, I had to do something tonight. They tried to kill Carissa. I'm at the hospital with Derrick and her now. She's gonna be okay. But I'm so scared. We miss you out here, girl. Please pull through! I love you."

What the fuck? Here I was, wallowing in my own self-pity, and my girl ended up in the hospital. I jumped into the shower, only because I had to. After spending three weeks in the house alone, I wouldn't have been any good to anybody—smelling the way I did. I threw on some brand-new cotton men's Gap sweatpants, a sweatshirt, and my Timberlands. Then I grabbed my .38 and my black North Face coat. I was on my way out the door, when I saw all three of my friends getting off the elevator. It had only been three weeks since I'd seen them, but it felt like ages. The moment they saw me, tears filled their eyes and mine too. We embraced each other before we walked into my bare apartment.

"Damn, girl," Kenyetta said. "You got rid of all your shit!"

"It looks like a brand-new apartment in here. All we gotta do now is paint," Mercedes said.

I didn't say anything. I just stared at the scar on Carissa's pretty face. I felt like shit for letting my girl down. She must've seen the hurt in my eyes.

"It's not your fault. It could've happened to any one of us," Carissa said. Even after she'd gone through something so traumatic, she was still trying to console me. I knew we were tougher than a lot of dudes, and Carissa just proved it.

"Yeah, but it didn't happen to one of us. It happened to you. I'm so sorry, Rissa," I said as I hugged her tightly.

I removed my coat and tossed it on the floor.

"Damn, girl! I thought I was lunchin' when I first saw your little pea head, but now I'm sure. You did lose a rack of weight," Carissa said.

"I was thinkin' the same thing," Mercedes said, giving me the once-over.

"So how much weight have you lost, anyway? You look good!" Kenyetta asked.

"She does!" Mercedes added. "She tryin' to hide that bangin'-ass body in that big-ass coat."

"I don't know. I haven't weighed myself, but I'm sure about twenty-five pounds."

"Yeah. I bet Thick would be all on that now," Kenyetta added.

When she said that, the laughter stopped. Just the mentioning of his name fucked the entire mood up and made my heart skip two beats. I realized even more how much I missed him, and still loved him. I guess it was too early, even after three weeks, to be fully over somebody.

"I'm sorry, girl. I hit a bob before coming up here, so I'm still sayin' stupid shit," Kenyetta apologized.

"Don't worry 'bout it," I said. "I'll get over his fat ass sooner or later."

"Well . . . we got a treat for you," Mercedes said as they looked at one another and smiled devilishly.

"Well, are y'all gonna stand there, lookin' stupid and shit, or are you gonna tell me what's up?"

Just then, Mercedes walked up to me and told me to hold out my hand. When I did it, she placed three diamond rings in my hand, one of which was an engagement ring. At first, I didn't know what I was looking at; but when I focused on the size of the rock in the engagement ring, I knew I'd seen it twice. Once at the Tiffany parking lot, and again when I was begging my man not to walk out of my life. So I knew exactly whose they were; I just wondered how they got 'em.

"How the fuck did y'all get these?" I laughed, observing them closely.

"Let's just say his pretty little girlfriend ain't pretty no more," Mercedes said.

157

"Yeah . . . a few days after that thing happened to Carissa, we blamed that bitch for it. We figured if Thick was in the picture, you wouldn't be all messed up and shit, and you would be on your job. So we took our frustrations out on her. I think Dyson and them know we had somethin' to do with it, but we been denying it." Kenyetta laughed.

"So what y'all robbed her or something?" I asked.

"Fuck no! What we look like robbing her ass? Her money can't fuck wit' ours! We sliced her fucking face up and took her rings as proof." Mercedes laughed.

"Is she alive?"

"Yep. But she paralyzed. And she will never look the same, that's for sure," Kenyetta added.

"Damn, y'all some fuckin' pit bulls!"

We laughed.

Mercedes said, "But you ain't heard the worst part."

"I didn't?"

"Naw . . . the bitch lied about being pregnant. She probably ruined your relationship over telling Thick some bullshit, and she wasn't even pregnant." Mercedes laughed.

That hurt. I was happy that my friends had handled business for me, because I would've done it for them. But knowing that my world had been ruined on the strength of a lie tore me apart inside.

My curiosity was piqued. "How do you know she lied about being pregnant?"

"Well . . . when Thick asked the doctor if his baby was gonna be okay, the doctor looked at him like he was fuckin' crazy. So he found out right then that, that bitch was a fuckin' liar!"

"So what he do?"

"Dropped a few g's for her hospital bill and left her ass stranded. He pissed 'bout that shit," Carissa added. "You know how bad he wants a kid."

"Yeah . . . that's why he loves Li'l C so much!" Mercedes added.

I knew I shouldn't be, but I was happy that his world had ended in a matter of seconds, like mine did. For some reason that news gave me the strength that I needed to resume my position in Emerald City. As far as I was concerned, he got exactly what he deserved.

"Well, what's going on with Emerald City?" I asked.

They were real quiet before answering. I could tell by the looks in their eyes that they needed me back, just as much as I needed them.

"Shit ain't been the same. I had to kill Key because him and his brothers were gettin' ready to rape Carissa. If it hadn't been for Derrick coming back, I don't know what would've happened," Mercedes said.

"Derrick?" I asked, not believing my ears.

159

"Yes. Derrick. He really looked out, girl," Mercedes said, smiling a little more than she should have.

"Them niggas got us fucked up!" I said, trying to wrap my mind around someone hurting one of my girls. "I'm just happy you're okay."

"Don't worry about it," Carissa said again. "I'm as tough as nails!"

"I know Lavelle flipped, didn't he?" I questioned.

"Yeah . . . but I already handled it!" Mercedes told me proudly. "But they did air out everybody else in that muthafucka just for not stopping it."

"So you finally got a body on your gun?" I giggled. "Look at you, tryin' to be gangsta."

"Naw . . . I'm not gangsta—I'm cute! But I will fuck somebody up about my girls."

It was silent for a minute in my apartment as I looked at all of them.

"Let's make a pact. We'll always have each other's back from this moment forward." I put my hand in the middle, and all of theirs covered mine.

"Nobody can break our bond!" Kenyetta said, looking at all of us.

"Nobody!" Mercedes and Carissa added.

Our hands dropped after we fortified our friendship.

"Well . . . now that that's out of the way, let's get shit back in order. I'm back now!"

Chapter 19

What's Up?

January, Saturday, 6:00 P.M.

Thick

Thick couldn't believe that Zakayla had lied to him about being pregnant.

He had plans to wife her and give her everything she wanted. He had already spent big money on the luxury apartment, the diamonds on her fingers, the clothes in her closet, and her truck. However, nothing proved his love more than dumping longtime girlfriend and business partner, Yvette. But after finding out she was nothing but a liar, he felt the only thing he owed to her was paying her hospital bills.

He was on his way to check out the affairs at Emerald City, when he noticed Yvette outside running business. He smiled a little because he hadn't seen her in weeks. What caught him off guard was not how she was putting niggas in check, and handling business, but how good she looked. He could tell she'd lost a lot of weight, and now she looked like she did when he first met her.

"I'm not tryin' to hear dat shit! Now you know your fuckin' hours, and I expect you to be on your job!" Yvette yelled as she grabbed the hood of his coat.

"Yvette, I missed three days, man. That was it!"

"I don't give a fuck. Since I been in charge of security, yo ass only been out of work one time. Now, all of a sudden, you need three days? Don't fuck wit' me, Veil! Now get back to work." She was scolding one of Harold's soldiers.

He walked off and did as he was told. The soldiers realized that unlike the other women, Yvette wouldn't waste no time putting somebody in check or pulling the trigger. Her feistiness and the weight she lost began to turn Thick on.

He parked his truck in front of Unit C and walked toward her. When Yvette saw Thick, she started off in the other direction. She wasn't prepared to see him. Not yet. He quickly grabbed her hand before she was able to make it up the stairs. He knew if she made it inside, her friends would be in her ear telling her to leave his sorry ass alone.

"Come here for a sec, Vette."

"I gotta go." She tried to pull away, but his grip was tight.

"Where you goin'?" he asked.

"Me and you ain't got nothin' to talk 'bout, Thick. It's over, remember?"

"Look . . . I fucked up, okay? I was wrong for even tryin' to play you. I let that bitch get in my head and I gotta live with the possibility of losing you. But I swear I'm ready to do right by you."

• His words heavy in passion caught her off guard, and she so desperately wanted to believe him. But deep in her heart, she knew she couldn't.

"Thick, why you doin' this to me? Please let me get on with my life." Tears ran down her face. "Do you know how hard it was for me to move on? Why can't you let me go?"

"Because I love you, that's why. Come talk to me in my truck," he said, trying to get her away from the watchful eyes of her friends.

"I can't, Thick." She attempted to walk away again.

"Yvette, please . . . just gimme one minute," he begged, looking into her eyes.

It was the first time, in a long time, she had heard the passion in his voice.

"Okay. Only for a minute," she conceded.

When she got into his truck, the familiar sight and smells snatched her back to a time when things were good with them. *Maybe we can work on it,* she thought. *Maybe he really does love me.*

When he came around to the driver's side of the car, he jumped in, closed the door, and pulled around the back of the building. The smell of the Touch cologne by Burberry he wore made her want to take him in her mouth. He let his five o'clock shadow come through and shaped it up, adding a distinguished look to a handsome thug. She couldn't help but stare at him and admire how sexy he made a pair of jeans, Timbs, black shirt, and Coogi jacket look.

Before she could say anything, he reached in and kissed her. For a minute she inhaled him; then she moved into his kisses. Her pussy began to throb as her heart was getting rid of what it had told her for the past few weeks. Here she was, smelling him, touching him; she didn't want it to end. Some kind of way, she managed to pull away from him—not wanting to give in too easy, not yet, anyway.

"What's wrong, baby?" he asked. "I said I was wrong for what I did to you. That bitch got in my head and fucked shit up. But I knew all along you were the woman for me. And I ain't neva lettin' that shit happen again. That's my word, baby," he said, touching her leg and sending chills through her.

"You hurt me, Thick. You hurt me bad. Do you know how it felt to see you walk arm in arm with another woman? You acted like you didn't even know me—like I had done something to you. You couldn't even spend five minutes to tell me why it was over between us."

"I know. But you know how much I been

wanting a baby. That bitch told me she was pregnant, and I fell for it."

"Yeah, but you cheated on me! With all the shit that happened, you making me forget about that. You cheated on me, Thick. She shoulda never been able to pretend to be pregnant, in the first fucking place!" Tears fell from her eyes.

"I know, baby. That's why I'm glad y'all fucked that bitch up. Otherwise, I'da married that scandalous ho."

"Thick, I didn't know nothing 'bout that," she said as she wiped the tears from her face. "Don't get me wrong, I'm glad she got what she deserved, but I didn't give the word on that shit either. I had made up my mind that you were gonna do what you wanted to do. And there was nothing I could do 'bout it."

She didn't want him thinking that she was so desperate to be with him that she gave the order.

"Well, whatever," he said. "I'm just glad it was done. But I do love you. Let's move on from this, and work on us, baby." He gently grabbed her face and kissed her lips.

Yvette's heart started to beat rapidly. When Thick moved his body close to hers, and then reached across her body to push her seat all the way back, the anticipation of making love to him consumed her. She didn't think he deserved her body, but she couldn't resist him either. It was like he owned her, as if she still belonged to him. He unbuttoned her coat and gripped her breasts. She gave in to his touches and confirmed her feelings by soft moans.

"I want to make love to you, baby. I miss this pussy so much. Remember how we used to make love in my truck? Let's take things back to the way they used to be."

His words sent a wave of rage over her as she remembered him sleeping with Zakayla in his truck. Her hate took over when she thought about how she begged him not to leave, and he played her in front of all of her friends.

"You love me?" she asked as she breathed heavily into his kisses.

"Yes, baby. I fuckin' love you, girl," he said. His mouth covered hers, and his dick was reaching full thickness.

She moaned into his mouth. "Do you need me?"

"Yes, baby, I need you. . . . I need you."

She pulled away, startling him. "Well, you should have thought about that before you walked out of my life. It's over. Go fuck that gimp in the hospital bed. I'm through wit' you!" She got out of the car, slammed the truck door, and ran toward the building.

After three unsuccessful attempts to get her to come back, Thick decided that he wasn't gonna be played. He noticed that in her rush to leave, she dropped her keys on his floorboards.

He picked them up and devised a cold plan that would mean death, and ending his friends' relationships with their women.

Thick pulled up on unsuspecting Critter in the alley behind Unit A. Even though it was dark, he knew the small-framed Critter anywhere. As high as he'd gotten over the years, Critter had never lost his glasses; and he always wore a dirty suit and dress coat, like he was still working for the government. Thick could tell he was trying to cop some dope, and the dealer he was talking to was giving him a hard time. *That nigga always want a freebie,* Thick thought. He knew his plan would work because Critter was fiending.

"Critter! Come here, man!" Thick yelled from his truck.

Critter moved as fast as he could to the truck, even though the withdrawals were making things hard on his body.

Critter immediately started explaining. "Hey, man, I ain't botherin' nobody. Honest."

"Calm down, nigga. I got a job for you. You wanna make a couple of bucks?"

"Yeah. Sure, man."

"Look . . . you gonna need some help. You got anybody that can help you bring some boxes down to my truck."

Critter looked around and saw Rod talking to

167

another fiend in the yard. He flagged him down and they both stood at the passenger side of Thick's truck. Thick told them that he needed them to get his box from A55, which was one of the stash houses in Unit A. Thick gave them Yvette's key and told them to get a box marked as "Thick's things." When they returned, he promised to give them dope and fifty dollars apiece.

Critter and Rod eagerly accepted the keys and hurried up to Unit A to get the box. With their judgment clouded, all they could think of was getting that dope and satisfying their high. When they got off the elevator, they ran down the hall toward A55. When they reached the door, Critter grabbed the key from his pocket and opened the door. Rod followed behind him and moved into the apartment.

The moment Kristina saw Critter and Rod coming through the door, she removed both of her guns from their holsters and unloaded multiple bullets into their body. Critter, although riddled with bullets, tried to crawl out of the apartment.

"Please . . . please don't kill me. Thick—"

Before he could get his sentence out, Kristina walked over, stood on top of him, and put two caps in his face.

When she was sure they were both dead, she picked up the keys off the floor and noticed they were Yvette's.

Afterward, she put in a call.

Chapter 20

What's Up?

January, Sunday, 11:45 A.M.

Cameron

"I'm tellin' you, this is some bullshit. Yvette would have never given Critter her set of keys. She must've dropped them or somethin', baby."

"You think I don't know that?" Cameron asked Mercedes in their bedroom.

"So what's gonna happen now?"

"We gonna have a meeting tonight. But you know shit is tight again, since we got those extra bodies on us. That's over three bodies in three weeks. Five-O gonna be on our shit hard."

"I know. Damn!"

"But don't worry 'bout nothin'." Cameron reached in and gave her a kiss. "As long as we have each otha, we straight."

"Is that right?" Mercedes smiled.

"That's right. Now you know I talked to my baby girl Chante, right?"

"Naw, you didn't tell me," Mercedes said as she rubbed his shoulders. "Well, what happened? Did you find out why her ass been cuttin' up in school?"

"Yep! She say we don't spend no time with her, for one. And for two, she said her friends been clownin' her about your moms fuckin' their grandpops behind their grandmas' backs."

"You lyin'! She said that?"

"I wish I was. So she felt she had to defend the family. So my li'l shawty was about to knife a muthafucka!"

"But the teacher, baby?"

"She said that bitch ain't do nothin' to help when she told her they were teasin' her. So she flipped on her ass. I don't blame her either." Cameron laughed.

"It's this area, baby. We got to get from around here," Mercedes said, looking at her engagement ring.

"We will." He kissed her ring. "Just as soon as we get married. But for now, we'll look into some private schools."

"Okay."

"And where's Li'l C? He been out the house more than me lately."

"Out there on the yard with his friends. Leave him alone, he just tryin' to be like you." She smiled.

170

"I know, right. My li'l nigga just like me." He stood up and put on his bulletproof vest. "Well, let me see what's up with this meeting. I'll let you know the status the moment I hear something."

"I love you." She reached in for a kiss.

"I love you more." He grabbed one of her nipples and squeezed it. "I'm fuckin' them walls up when I get back tonight."

"Promises, promises."

"And look. Tell Yvette everything will be okay and to keep her head up. We in this thing together."

"I will. But we all feelin' fucked up 'bout Critter. Kristina had to do what she had to do, but he really looked out for us."

"I know, baby." He hugged her. "But business is business, and he ain't had no business bein' in our stash house either."

"You right."

"Well, I'm on my way to this meeting. Keep my plate warm and my pussy tight," he said as he left.

"What you sayin', Thick? Cuz what you tellin' me don't make no fuckin' sense, man!" Cameron yelled at the emergency meeting held at Thick's mother's place, off Minnesota Avenue in the Northeast.

"I'm sayin' that Yvette put our entire operation in jeopardy by wearin' her feelings on her sleeve, man. And if Kristina hadn't been on point, who knows how much money we woulda been into Dreyfus for?" Thick asked as he drank Absolut Pears on the rocks.

"I understand why you may be upset, but I'm in love with Carissa, man. We been lookin' at new places to live and everything. Last week we put a deposit down on a new apartment out in Forestville, Maryland. So what you tellin' me now don't even make no sense," Lavelle said.

"And when were you gonna tell us you were takin' one of the girls out of Emerald?" Thick asked.

"Soon," Lavelle said, realizing his oversight.

"That's the kinda shit I'm talkin' about. This entire operation is fallin' the fuck apart!"

Thick was unsympathetic with his friends and their reasoning for not wanting to end their relationships. He felt what needed to be done *needed to be done,* even if he was the one who had set up Yvette. For his own selfish reasons, he wanted them to end their relationships with their girlfriends, and pledge loyalty to Emerald City—and Emerald City only. But what he hadn't expected was so much resistance, especially considering a few of them slept with other women on a regular basis, the same way he did.

He hit his fist on the table and walked around it, eyeing each of the members of the squad. "Listen . . . what would have happened if it had been somebody else runnin' up in the house? Dreyfus woulda come in blazin' just like he did on Tyland! And here y'all are sittin' here, cryin' over some bitches, who'll probably leave y'all asses in a couple of months, anyway! Now, if y'all are loyal to anything, other than Emerald City, let me know. Cuz right now, I'm confused. Maybe we'll have to revisit who'll be runnin' things in Emerald City."

"And what the fuck is that supposed to mean?" Dyson asked as he stood up.

"Just what the fuck I said!" Thick shot back. "Now I want to know right here and right fuckin' now, what the fuck do y'all plan to do? Pledge loyalty to Emerald City by ending your relationships with the bitches—that could ruin us—and focus on business at hand?" He paused. "Or go on with what you doin' and risk somethin' worse happenin', the next time one of them gets mad?"

The room fell silent.

Thick asked, "By a show of hands, who's in and who's out? The time is now."

No one made a move until Dyson drank from his cup, wiped his hand on his jeans, and looked at his brothers in blood, sweat, and tears. Then he raised his hand.

"I pledge loyalty to y'all," Dyson said.

Thick looked around the room, placed his gun on the table, and said, "I'll lay down my life for every one of you muthafuckas!"

After that, Cameron and Lavelle both looked at one another, searching for who would first betray the women they loved. Because unlike the others, they intended to place the women in their lives on their arms. Lavelle quickly swallowed all of the drink in his glass and poured another glass. With as much hesitation and hurt as a man who didn't want to walk away from someone he loved could muster, he reluctantly raised his hand.

"I pledge loyalty to my brothers too. Don't let me down."

Cameron was fucked up when Lavelle folded, because he realized he was the only other person, outside of himself, who loved his woman. But Cameron also knew the day would one day come when he, too, would have to choose. But he never knew it would happen so soon. So without wasting any more time, he made his decision.

"I pledge 'Honor, Loyalty, Obedience, and Silence to the Emerald City Squad,' always."

For the next hour of the meeting, they devised a plan that would keep the women in office permanently, and dissolve their relationships completely over the next six months. They figured if they'd gotten used to working for them— as opposed to being in a relationship—nothing like what had happened to Yvette would happen again. They were convinced by what Thick was telling them: they would be able to convince the

174

women that a strictly business relationship was best for everyone.

Thick didn't share with them his own selfish motives for wanting them to end their relationships. All he ever wanted was control—control over everything. He wanted control over Yvette; and when he couldn't get it, he ran to Zakayla. He wanted control over Zakayla; but when he felt she betrayed him, he left her stranded and tried to run back to Yvette. But when Yvette saw right through him, he plotted against her.

But Thick's evil plot had started long ago, when he wanted control over Emerald City, so he placed the order to have Dex and his wife, Stacia, killed.

At this point all he wanted to do was run Emerald City and reap its benefits. . . .

No matter who he had to hurt in the process.

Three
Hard, Long
Weeks
Later

Chapter 21

Still True

February, Saturday, 9:15 A.M.

Doctanian

Doctanian was inside his girlfriend's wet pussy.

He was trying desperately not to reach an orgasm so quickly; but ever since she became pregnant, the walls of her pussy became tighter and hotter. Prior to now, he always thought it was just a rumor that pregnant pussy felt so good.

He was stroking Jordan's pussy repeatedly when he felt his self sliding into a euphoric orgasm.

He let out a moan. "I'm cummin', baby."

"Come on, daddy. Cum inside this wet pussy," she urged. "I want to feel you inside me."

Without saying another word, Doctanian let himself go as he oozed all of his cum inside her heated pussy. When he pulled out, Jordan lifted her body and placed his warm dick inside her mouth.

"Ummm, I love to taste you after you've been inside me."

It was this type of thing that made him obsess over Jordan. While she had him still inside her mouth, sucking him as if she was licking a piece of candy, her cell phone rang, as it had done several times earlier in the day. He started to ignore it, but on instinct he reached on the nightstand to give it to her to prevent Jordan from straining her pregnant body by grabbing it herself. She jumped up and snatched it out of his hand.

"I got it!" she said as she ran to the bathroom and closed the door behind her.

"Okay. If it's one of your little friends, tell 'em thanks for fuckin' shit up!" He laughed as he lay on the bed, naked and satisfied.

He was in love with her in every sense of the word. Now after five months of her being pregnant, he was preparing to propose to her and move her out of Emerald City before the baby was born.

Doctanian jumped up and knocked on the door after realizing Jordan was still on the phone twenty minutes later. He wasn't trying to be jealous, but he thought lately her behavior was sort of weird. When she came out, he asked her if everything was okay. She brushed him off and said it was a friend who had something going on with her family. After taking one look at her beautiful naked body, and the belly that was carrying his baby, he melted instantly.

"I'm sorry, shawty. Let me get out of here and make some cash so I can get you out this hood."

"No problem, daddy," Jordan said as she kissed him, sucking gently on his bottom lip. "I got a little treat for you when you come back over."

Doctanian got dressed and left Jordan's apartment in Emerald City, which she shared with her mother, who was also his customer.

Doctanian wasn't sure at first, but after a while he was positive he saw Li'l C serving somebody. This bothered him because although he put in work for his father, he always hoped Li'l C would stand clear of the game. When the customer left, Doctanian hurried over to him before he got a chance to serve anybody else.

"Ay, man! What you doin' out here?"

"Same thing you doin'!" Li'l C said as he pulled down his cap and added his money in his pile.

"But why you doin' it? Your family already paid."

"Cuz I want my own dough! You live off your folks?"

"Naw! But if they were livin' it up like yours, and I was still a youngin', I damn sure would be."

"Well, everything ain't what it look like," Li'l

C said in a low voice. "My folks ain't together no more. They don't think I know, but I do. Anyway . . . I'm old enough to make my own way now."

Doctanian didn't like hearing Li'l C talking like he was, but he figured it would happen sooner or later if his parents didn't get a better grip on him.

"Listen, li'l nigga, what ever happened to you bein' that video director we talked 'bout?" Doctanian asked.

"Naw. I changed my mind. My friends think that's wack."

"That's cuz they some pussies. Only pussies would think being a video director is wack. Do you realize how many women you'd be around any given day?" Doctanian asked as he play punched him in the face. "This life ain't for you, man."

"Why not? You do it," Li'l C asked.

Doctanian didn't know what to say, because at this point in his life, he was living fucked up. He hated serving dope and seeing the effects it took every day on customers' bodies. His mother's words haunted him every day, when she told him that what he was doing was wrong. And although she didn't think he was listening, he was. But he was saving his money to move his girlfriend, baby, and mother out of the hood eventually. To him it was just a matter of time.

"You right. I ain't neva lied to you, and I ain't

gonna start now. So let's do this. You become a big-time video director and I'll produce you. We'll be like them punk-ass niggas Jay-Z and Dame Dash was."

Li'l C looked up in the air as though seriously thinking about his offer. And then the same smile came across his face that Doctanian had seen before—the one when Doctanian was sure he'd won Li'l C over. Looking at him, Doctanian wished it were as easy for him to believe in dreams as it still was for Li'l C. No matter what, Doctanian made up his mind to keep any promise to Li'l C that he made—just as long as the young boy took the offer and stayed out of the game.

"Okay! We got a deal!" Li'l C said as he gave him five.

"All right! But I don't wanna see you out here no more, unless you comin' to see me."

"I know, man! Stop sweatin' me."

"Ahh, man. Before you go, I want to know somethin'."

"What, man?" Li'l C asked.

"Who put you on, anyway?"

Li'l C turned around and said, "Uncle Thick."

Doctanian couldn't believe his ears.

Chapter 22

The Meeting

February, Saturday, 6:00 P.M.

Yvette

After three weeks I was finally able to convince my girls to go out with me on a night on the town.

After they said no to dancing, we settled for drinks, instead. And when we stepped out, we looked like we were getting ready to shoot a music video. We were dressed in fatigues and different color wife beaters, and we all were wearing makeup. Every dude in there was trying to holla the moment we walked through the bar.

"So what's this 'bout, Yvette?" Mercedes asked me, after we'd been relaxing at our table for a minute. "You been askin' us out for a while now, and now we're here and you ain't sayin' nothin'."

"I'm just happy to see y'all, that's all. Plus I

wanted you to get some liquor up in you before I get down to business."

"Well, if you don't mind, I'd like to get down to business now," Carissa said.

"Me too," Mercedes added.

"May I take your orders now? Or would you like refills on your drinks?" the waitress asked.

We were posted up at the Dave and Buster's in White Flint. I was able to reserve the private room for us at the last minute, because I felt what needed to be said had to be done in private.

"Yes, please. Bring everybody a double of everything. And come back for our orders later."

"No problem," she said as she walked off, eyeing the five crisp hundred-dollar bills already lying on the table.

"So what's up, girl?" Mercedes asked.

"Okay. Has anybody noticed a difference in the guys?" I asked in a low voice as I sipped on my vodka martini.

They looked around at one another, and then back at me. Carissa decided to speak first.

"Have we noticed a change in the guys? Is that some kind of fuckin' trick question or somethin'?"

"No, it's not, Rissa. I'm very serious."

"If you consider Lavelle not coming home, and tellin' me he don't know about the relationship anymore—*after he's all I known*—different, hell yes! Or if you call him comin' by checkin' on me like he's my fuckin' manager instead of my boyfriend, then yes! I consider that different too. Or if you call bein' different, him comin' by kissin' the girls and ignorin' the hell out of me, then I guess we got somethin' too! So you tell me, Yvette, what do you fuckin' think?" she screamed as Kenyetta rubbed her gently on the back, trying to hold back her own tears.

"Yvette, you're our girl and we love you. But we have business to run at Emerald City, so we need to know what's up. Askin' stuff like this is only makin' matters worse. If you got somethin' to say, just say it. Be real with us. Whatever it is, we can handle it," Kenyetta said as she handed Carissa a napkin for her tears.

"I think they planned this," I finally said, looking at all of them. I wanted to see if they felt anything remotely similar to what I felt.

Mercedes asked, "Planned what?"

"I think they planned to dump us. Now, I don't know 'bout Thick. I believe in my heart that nigga was doin' what the fuck he was doin', anyway. But you not goin' to tell me that Lavelle is gonna up and leave you, Carissa, and that all of a sudden, Cameron, who loves your dirty drawers, girl, will all of a sudden leave you too, at the same time!"

"But what sense does that make?" Mercedes insisted.

"Exactly. It makes no fuckin' sense! All of this is some bullshit! We laid our lives on the line.

No, scratch that! We *lay* our lives on the line *every fuckin' day for them niggas*! And them mutha-fuckas swore that this shit would never be permanent, and that they'd come back for us when it was all said and done. And what did they do? Dump us at the first sign of trouble."

When I looked around at my sisters' faces, I could tell I was getting to them, and I decided to hit the hammer on the nail.

"I believe what happened between me and Thick triggered everythin'. I believe by me abandoning Emerald City, that gave them the impression that we couldn't handle a relationship and business at the same time."

"This ain't your fault, girl," Kenyetta said.

"I didn't say that," I said. "I don't believe this is any of our faults. I believe we're victims of our love to niggas who didn't deserve it. And I believe we played the fool for men who promised to protect us and didn't."

When the waitress returned with our drinks, I advised her that she was very helpful, but unless we called her back, we wouldn't be needing her anymore for the rest of the night. I didn't want any other witnesses around for what was about to be said.

"So what's up, girl? We've been knowin' you far too long. Somethin's gotta be up. What's your plan?" Kenyetta asked.

"I say we overthrow them and take over Emerald City."

It was so silent now the only sound that could be heard was the crowd in the game room. I was surprised, because although I would've never thought about betraying my man, in my mind I still knew we could run Emerald City alone if we needed. We were doing it, anyway, but their silence only proved to me that they didn't feel the same.

"Do you know what you're sayin'?" Carissa asked.

"You damn right I do!"

"We can't do that?" Carissa laughed as she threw back both of her drinks. "Can we?"

"Why not?" Mercedes asked, looking around the table. "Why can't we?"

That's what I'm talkin' about! My girls are finally waking up! I thought proudly.

"I was thinkin' the same thing," Kenyetta added. "We've been runnin' Emerald City all along, anyway. And since them muthafuckas want to carry it like that, let 'em get carried!"

"There go my muthafuckin' girls!" I smiled.

"What 'bout Dreyfus? He got a relationship wit' them?" Carissa asked.

"Dreyfus has a relationship wit' his money. The only thing he worried 'bout is gettin' paid. He don't care 'bout nothin' else. Anyway, you think he don't know we're the gatekeepers? You think if somethin' happened to Emerald City's stash, he wouldn't come to us first?" I asked.

"She right 'bout that shit! He'd walk over our bodies to get to theirs." Mercedes laughed.

"But he's the connect. How can we use the connect—"

I cut Carissa off and answered all her questions at once. I had already quarterbacked the entire thing before I even came to them. There's one thing I didn't like to do, and that was come to a meeting with a bunch of bullshit. I always came prepared and with a plan in mind. Thick taught me that.

"This is how it's goin' down," I said as they all moved in to listen. "The first thing we do is move out of Emerald City."

"But they'll know somethin's up," Carissa said.

"No, they won't. Just like Yvette moved all of her shit, without movin' shit out the building, that's the same way we can move," Kenyetta said. "I don't need shit in that apartment."

"Speak for yourself, bitch." Mercedes laughed. "I need my fur coats."

I told them my plan. "Well, this is what we do. We take as much stuff by hands as we can. No boxes and no trash bags. Then we keep the apartments. They'll come in handy later. Trust me. We change the locks too, because them niggas got keys. We want them cut the fuck off."

"I'm likin' this shit more and more already," Kenyetta said in a devious tone.

"Once we're moved out, we give away testers

for the entire week the guys go away to Vegas. This will force us to have to contact Dreyfus to get more supply. At this point Mercedes and I will meet with Dreyfus and build a rapport. It'll be us because Mercedes is familiar with the weight, since she collects the money from the lieutenants, and I'm in charge of security.

"Once we make him comfortable, we'll get in good with the lieutenants and the soldiers. We'll feel out who's who. Now I already predict they'll be a problem with two of the lieus and their soldiers. They're too loyal to the niggas. If we have to, we'll kill 'em. Does anybody got a problem with that?"

"Wit' what?" Carissa asked.

"Murder."

"I'll die for y'all," Carissa said.

"I'll die for y'all too," Kenyetta said.

"I already killed a muthafucka, so it ain't nothin' but a thang," Mercedes bragged.

Everyone laughed.

"I ain't gotta say shit, because y'all know I'll lay a muthafucka on their backs twice quick for my girls. So if we ain't got no problem with that, it's all good. When the niggas come back from Vegas, there will be some drama, believe that. But they got other shops. So if they're smart, they can gracefully bow down. Plus we'll have our soldiers already rearranged and ready for war."

Chapter 23

Greed

February, Friday, 7:34 P.M.

Jordan

"Come on, Jordan! What the fuck you waitin' on?" Erick yelled.

"I ain't neva done nothin' like this before, Erick. You gotta give me some more time." She was crying on the cell phone in her room, hoping no one could hear the dirt she was planning against the one man who loved her more than himself.

"You ain't gotta do nothin' but have his ass come to your house. Me and my boys doin' the rest. If anythin', you lookin' out for your man, so we won't put this lead in him!"

"*My* boy and *your* lieutenant," she reminded him while sitting on her bed.

"Fuck that shit! Ain't nobody bossin' me

around. Shit gonna start changin' for real. I just need you to do what we agreed on."

"But . . . but then he'll lose his position as lieutenant. They'll know he let somebody get into the building and that he wasn't on watch." Jordan sniffed as she began to gather the covers in a bunch between her legs, wiping her tears with them.

"Listen, Jordan. Emerald City is gettin' ready to fold, anyway. You ain't notice Thick and 'em ain't been around here lately?"

"Yeah, but—"

"But what?" he shot back, getting upset that she was wasting too much time. "I got connects set up at Tyland Towers, where if this goes through, I'm gonna be lieutenant and maybe even captain. And if you do this, you'll be securing Doc's future, so he won't have to mop no floors at Walmart. Think about your baby!"

"I am!" she yelled. "That's why I'm scared!"

Erick was in Jordan's ear hard. He had been trying to convince her for over two weeks to help him get Doctanian to leave his shift early, which was something he never did. Erick knew that it was just a matter of time before the stash houses changed again. Because he didn't have his connect who told him where the new houses moved, once this one changed again, he wouldn't know any more information. And if that happened, he couldn't plot to rob another house.

He needed Jordan's help in the worst way if

this was gonna work right. Erick knew that the lieutenants operated the front of the units with the soldiers; therefore, only one soldier manned a stash house inside the building during shop hours. This was because extra security was already outside the building and was deemed unnecessary. So his plan was to first send unsuspecting dummies ahead of him to break inside the stash house.

Whoever was on guard would eradicate them immediately, but the soldier wouldn't see Erick coming or the bullet he'd place in his head. In order for his plan to work, it had to be done before shop hours ended, because they increased security afterward with three or four soldiers guarding at a time.

"Okay." Jordan sniffled. "How much you giving me again?" she asked. She was hurt, but not enough *not* to claim the money he said he'd give her.

"You funny. I'm gonna give you four g's. Like I said." He laughed, feeling comfortable that she was going to help him again.

"Okay . . . but don't hurt my baby's father. If you don't see him walkin' toward my buildin', call this shit off!" Jordan demanded.

"Your baby daddy, huh? Now that's funny. How you know you ain't carryin' my kid around in there?"

His words caused Jordan to press the end button on her cell phone; then she threw it across her room against her bedroom door. She always thought he could possibly be the father, but the thought alone was as disgusting as Doctanian not being the father. She only slept with Erick because he was aggressive and cocky; and at times that turned her on. But when the sex was over, she always wished she hadn't shared her body with him, because he was always so rude and disrespectful to her. With Doc she had a future; with Erick she knew she'd have nothing.

Having heard the thump against her daughter's bedroom door, Jordan's mother, Da'vanta, walked into the room without knocking—something Jordan hated—and asked her what was wrong.

"Ma, get outta here!" Jordan yelled, trying to prevent her from seeing her red face, which was streaked from crying just moments before.

"You okay, baby?" she asked, trying to soften her up, so she could hopefully cop some dope from Doctanian later if he was coming over. Doctanian fed her needs sometimes, but he started to hate it, considering she was his girlfriend's mother.

"Yeah, Ma! Please leave! I want to be alone."

"You sure, baby? Want me to make you some tea or somethin'?" she asked, rubbing her arms.

"No, get outta here!"

Da'vanta was on her way out the door when she bent her frail body down to pick up her daughter's ringing cell phone. She became instantly upset when she noticed it was Erick's name across the display. She handed it to her daughter, who snatched it out of her hands instantly and demanded that she leave her room.

"Ma, get out!"

"I'm still your mother!" she said as she slammed the door and walked to her dark, dim living room, wondering when her next fix would come.

Da'vanta hated Erick because she felt he had something to do with the only man she ever loved being killed. But the love of her life was also responsible for getting her hooked on dope.

She couldn't help but cry as she thought about Critter.

Chapter 24

Loyalty

February, Saturday, 9:18 P.M.

Doctanian

In the past Doctanian had been kidnapped and held at gunpoint; yet, he never felt any fear like what he felt right now.

Upon receiving the news that his girlfriend, Jordan, might be having a miscarriage, he ran to his most trusted soldier, Erick, and asked him to hold down the fort, while he saw about the love of his life.

"Look, man! I need you to look afta things real quick!" Doctanian said as he tried to prevent himself from breaking down. "I gotta go handle somethin' now!"

"No problem, man. Everything cool?" Erick asked, curious as to what lie Jordan told him to have him so shook.

"Naw, man. Between me and you, my girl may

be havin' a miscarriage. I don't know what I'ma do if she loses the baby. I love them more than I love myself! That's my word!" Doc said, trying to hold back how he felt, although it showed through stronger than any words he could say.

Miscarriage? Erick thought. *Damn, that bitch is good!*

"I got you, man," he said while placing his hand on Doc's back. "I got these niggas out here. Go and take care of you and yours. Shit is all good out here! I got these niggas on lock. Trust!" Erick said as he convinced Doc to abandon his post.

With that, Doctanian ran toward his girl-friend's building. *Sucker-for-love–ass nigga!* Erick thought as he gave the word to the others that the plan was being carried out.

Out of breath and worried, Doc banged on Jordan's door. When her mother answered, he was angry that she didn't appear to be as worried as a mother whose daughter was having a miscarriage should be.

"What's wrong, Doc?" Da'vanta asked, sensing his eagerness to get in.

"Where's Jordan?" he asked as he pushed his way through the door and into Jordan's room.

"She ain't here," Da'vanta said. "I woke up and she was gone."

"She didn't tell you she was having a miscarriage?" he asked as he walked back into the living room with her. "She didn't say anything to you?"

"A *miscarriage*? No. She didn't say anything to me about havin' no miscarriage."

His mind was on overload as he assumed the ambulance had come and rushed his girlfriend out of the house. While she was talking, he looked around for signs of disruption. He decided to calm down and question Da'vanta thoroughly. Maybe she'd seen more than she realized; but due to smoking dope, she needed a jolt to make her remember.

"Ms. Porter, I'm worried 'bout Jordan. I need you to tell me everything that happened when she was here. Don't leave out nothin', because this is very important."

Da'vanta realized that unlike any other boy her daughter had dated, Doc genuinely cared about Jordan.

"Okay . . . well . . . ," she said as she sat on the sofa. "Earlier she was in her room upset. I came in and saw her cell phone on the floor."

Doc's heart raced as he imagined her in pain, and him not being there for her.

"So I came in and asked her what was wrong and if I could do anything for her." She rubbed her temples and then the sides of her arms, and then sat without speaking anymore.

"And what else, Ms. Porter?" he demanded, attempting to jolt her as she nodded off. "Ms. Porter, what else?"

"Oh . . . I'm sorry. And Erick," she said, coming out of a dope-induced nod. "Erick called and she took the call."

Doctanian backed up against the thirty-two-inch TV on the stand, knocking it over. The most treacherous thought imaginable ran through his mind. It sounded like his girlfriend—his child's mother—was possibly setting him up.

He tried to run to the door, but he was slowed by the pain in his heart and the knots in his stomach. Feeling loyalty to Emerald City, and being a true lieutenant, he decided to face his mistake head-on—even if it meant losing his position or even his life.

He pulled out his cell phone and contacted the one person he knew could hustle up the manpower needed to prevent whatever was getting ready to happen.

And that was Yvette.

Chapter 25

Can't Please Everybody

January, Saturday, 6:00 P.M.

Thick

The Vegas night sky was a brilliant mixture of oranges and reds preparing for the sunset.

People were just waking up from their naps, eager to stay up until the sun started all over again. No matter how much glitz and glamour was surrounding the Emerald City Squad, there was still obvious tension in the air, causing the atmosphere to be constantly on edge.

"I don't understand why you would invite that bum bitch!" Lavelle yelled at Thick in the hallway of his suite at the Bellagio. "I don't fuck wit' that girl at all like that."

The squad had reserved four rooms, with an extra room for the girls Thick had decided to bring with them from the city. Thick called himself "helping his friends" to get over Mercedes and Carissa, but Lavelle was growing irritated. Sharonda was in her room, while Shannon stayed up under them in the hopes of catching any stray bills falling to the floor.

The squad was there mainly for business, because Thick had convinced them that it wasn't cool to live under the fear of Dreyfus any longer. Several attempts by Dreyfus to take down their stash houses in the past would cause them more problems than it was worth.

Thick was also tired of dealing with him on consignment for the weight he needed to keep the city moving. Although Dreyfus had made it clear that he'd be willing to accept his money up front, the squad had gotten used to the modest time frame he allowed to pay his money back, even though it came with a jump in the price.

Thick was given the name of a Cuban connect, who agreed to meet with the squad after hearing how easy they moved weight in Emerald City. The connect offered to supply the weight at an affordable rate up front, and transport it safely to the city. After hearing this news, the fellas agreed that as long as they would be able to pay Dreyfus off, and sever the relationship on good terms, they'd be willing to meet Thick's connect.

"I thought you were feelin' her, yo! I was tryin' to cheer up your punk ass, because I'm tired of slippin' on your slob. You niggas been cryin' for three weeks and you startin' to bring me down!" he said as he walked into the living room, where Cameron was receiving a shoulder massage by Shannon, Derrick's jump-off.

"Man, I'm not tryin' to be stuck in Vegas with Sharonda's ass all week. I fuck wit' her when I get ready to, and leave it at that. Anyway, I thought the main purpose of this trip was business. They shouldn't even be here," Lavelle said, placing his nickel-plated .45 on the table.

"Look . . . we can leave them bitches down here, for all I give a fuck. It don't make me no neva-mind," Thick said as he shrugged his shoulders and lit the blunt, acting like Sharonda's friend Shannon wasn't even in the room. "I was just lookin' out for y'all cryin'-ass niggas."

"Man, ain't nobody tryin' to leave them hoes down here," Lavelle said as he brushed off what he considered to be a dumb-ass comment.

He didn't want to be bothered, but he wasn't trying to carry no females like that, especially considering he had daughters and wouldn't want anybody treating them badly. He just didn't want his entire week ruined in Vegas.

"All I'm sayin' is, bringin' them females down here ain't gonna make me move or work no quicker," Lavelle said as he pulled on the blunt that Thick handed him. "All she gonna do is make me mad."

Cameron wasn't saying much. He didn't understand why Thick invited the girls either. But after being up under a woman who took care of her body, and was as soft as Shannon, he was good for now. Still, nobody could get his mind off Mercedes; he didn't care how good the pussy was.

"Yeah, but maybe it'll help you get over that bitch!" Thick laughed as Cameron took time from his shoulder massage, to see what Lavelle's response would be.

"Be careful, nigga, that *bitch* you talkin' 'bout is still my daughter's mother. And if you call out her name again, my loyalty to Emerald City ends here," Lavelle said as he put his finger on the table, which was close to his gun.

"You's a funny nigga." Thick laughed as he walked toward the door that connected the rooms and popped his collar. "Y'all niggas so in love, y'all green. As long as it don't fuck wit' my business, it's all good."

He walked into his room and stuck his head back out the door. "Shannon!" he barked.

"Yes," she answered, looking up from Cameron's neck to see what he needed.

"Come here."

Without saying another word, she disappeared into the room with Thick and closed the door behind her. . . .

Leaving Cameron alone.

Chapter 26

Strapped

January, Saturday, 9:35 P.M.

Derrick

"We got the back secure. I'm turning off this phone so it won't go off when we rush they asses in the hallway. Y'all ready?" Derrick asked Yvette on the walkie-talkie they used for emergency purposes only.

"Born ready, nigga!"

Derrick grabbed four of his best soldiers, strapped with Glocks, Uzis, and TEC-9's, to secure the back of Unit B, which was the building Doctanian manned. Doctanian had sent them to make sure everything was okay, after he had spoken to Jordan's mother. Something didn't sit with him right, and he wanted them to make sure.

Creeping up the steps quickly, but quietly,

they had their guns in full view and ready to unload. An old lady trying to meet her friends on the third floor for a game of bingo was entering from the fourth floor. She almost passed out when she saw them creeping up the stairs dressed all in black. There was no need to tell her not to say anything about what she'd seen, because they'd already seen her face. Running back from where she came, she gave her apologies for disturbing them, and then disappeared.

The stash house was in Unit B, on the eighth floor. Any other time walking up the steps would have taken an immediate toll on Derrick's crew, considering they weren't aerobic cats. But tonight they didn't need to be fit, to do what needed to be done. They were running strictly off adrenaline.

As they approached the eighth floor, their hearts were pounding with the anticipation of what was in store. Far from being punks, his soldiers were ready to unleash on his command, and only *his* command. When Derrick heard footsteps, he placed his finger over his mouth, quieting them.

When they stopped moving, they realized that in the stairwell above them were two sets of footsteps that sounded as if they were moving in their direction. Suddenly they stopped, when a door opened, and a third set of steps became present.

Someone spoke. "What the fuck y'all doin', man?"

Derrick believed it was Doctanian's right-hand man, Erick.

"What you talkin' 'bout, we—"

Erick cut him off. "I don't want to hear that shit! Y'all some thievin'-ass niggas! And I can't stand thievin'-ass niggas."

"What the . . . I'm confused as shit, man. You need to tell me what the fuck is goin' on." The other voice echoed in the hallway. "We did everything—"

Before he could complete his statement, Derrick heard a bullet swirl from the barrel of what sounded like a .45 automatic weapon.

An anxious voice yelled out, "What the fuck you doin', man? Why you kill him like that?"

To see what was going on, Derrick instructed his troops to run full speed up the steps, ready to lay down everybody, if need be. When they reached the area where the voices were, they saw Ice, one of Doctanian's soldiers, pointing a gun at the back of Erick's head. The noise from them running up the stairs gave Ice the distraction he needed to catch Erick off guard and take his weapon.

Erick knew they were coming, when he had walked to Unit C and had seen Derrick's boys manning the station, instead of the girls. They hardly ever left their post. Immediately he went to plan B to protect his name. The only reason he went over to Unit C in the first place was to be seen *before* he robbed the stash house. But he was glad he did. He figured if something went down, the girls could vouch that he wasn't involved. But when he didn't see them manning the post, he knew word had gotten out that somebody was trying to infiltrate. So he hustled over to the building, not wanting his co-conspirators to be caught alive.

"Put your fuckin' gun down, slim!" Ice yelled at Erick.

Erick complied and put his hands up in the air.

"Them too. Tell them to put their fuckin' guns down!" Ice yelled.

"We ain't puttin' shit down, so you can get that out your fuckin' head," Derrick said as he gave the signal to buck that nigga when he gave the okay. "Now I want to know what the fuck is goin' on!" Derrick asked, eyeing Tonio's dead body.

"He a thief!" Erick interjected. He didn't care if he shot him or not, he still didn't want anybody knowing the part he took in everything.

"If I'm a thief, yo ass is a thief too, nigga, believe that! You tryin' to set me up or somethin', Erick? Yeah. That's what you do," Ice said as he began to talk like a maniac. "This nigga's tryin to set me up."

"You talkin' shit, nigga!" Erick screamed, realizing that his chances were better with calling Ice a liar and living than to take the beef that he was trying to rob the stash house too. Erick realized that if they found out he was in on it, he was going to die.

"I'm talkin' shit? I'm talkin' shit, nigga?" Ice yelled as he pushed the barrel of the gun toward his head, forcing Erick against the wall. His back was facing the closed door behind him.

"I don't know 'bout him talkin' shit, but you definitely are!" Yvette said as she busted through the sixth-floor door and unleashed a .45 bullet inside Ice's skull. "I'm tired of these niggas fuckin' wit' my money," she said as she wiped the blood off her mouth with the back of her hand and looked at Derrick.

She had seen everything from the small glass window in the door and had waited patiently for the moment to pull the trigger.

"That was some sexy-ass shit, shawty!" Derrick said as he put down his weapon, while instructing his soldiers to stay on guard.

"Thanks, baby. I'm glad you liked it." She winked, tucking her weapon in the back of her pants.

Suddenly Derrick smiled when he saw gun barrels sticking out, as if Charlie's Angels were coming through the doorway. His heart dropped when he saw Mercedes in a ski mask move into the hallway, with Carissa and Kenyetta following. They only put their weapons down when they saw Derrick's boy was still pointing at Erick. Derrick knew it was Mercedes because although she had on the ski mask, her ponytail peeked through, with the streaked golden blond hair that he liked.

"So it was true, huh?" Mercedes asked, removing her ski mask and revealing her beautiful face. "Some niggas were tryin' to get us again?"

"Hold fast," Yvette said. "We ain't out the woods yet. What's the deal with this nigga?" Yvette asked Derrick as she looked at Erick.

"I don't know yet. Let's ask him," he said, turning his attention to Erick. "What's your story? What you doin' here, man?"

"I got word that somebody was tryin' to steal from the house," he said, huffing and puffing, pretending he was out of breath. "So I came to see 'bout it."

"Is that right?" Yvette asked, doubting every word he said. "And how the fuck you know where the house was at?"

Erick was so shook that he didn't stop to think about that before he ran off his mouth. He thought quickly as Derrick's soldiers were ready to give the orders to end his life. "I came lookin' for Doc. His girl hit me up, sayin' he wasn't there yet. When I did, I saw Derrick's soldiers at Unit C, and they told me y'all went to see 'bout something over here."

"Which nigga was that?" Derrick asked, making mental notes to check out later whoever it was.

"I can't remember, man. It all happened so fast. You can ask 'em, though."

"Oh, we will," Derrick promised.

"Well, I'm hearin' different stories," Yvette added. "I'm hearin' you fuckin' wit' Doctanian's bitch and y'all tried to set us up."

Figuring that word must've gotten out that he talked to Jordan, he concocted another lie. He wasn't worried about Jordan vouching for his story, he had already pumped lead in her body and had stuffed her in the Dumpster around back. He had made a promise on the night CJ and Charles were killed that he would never leave witnesses, and he wanted to keep it that way.

"Like I said . . . Jordan called me, tryin' to contact Doc because he wouldn't answer his phone. Y'all know we used to kick it way back when, and she still has my number. Ain't nothin' else to it, I swear!"

When it was obvious that they didn't believe him, he went a bit further. "Y'all can ask her right now." He continued his alibi, throwing up his hands for added effect.

Since the call placed to Yvette from Doctanian indicated that something was not right, they decided to let him go. But Derrick promised to finish him later, if he found out anything different, and Erick had a feeling Derrick had every intention of keeping his promise.

Once again, Erick got away.

Chapter 27

Closing the Deal

February, Wednesday, 3:45 P.M.

Mercedes

Driving three hours to Dreyfus's compound in Virginia gave me some extra time to clear my mind and prepare for what needed to be done.

My goal was to convince the biggest dealer in D.C. that he should stop doing business the way he had been, and should start doing things differently.

Yvette was able to get the number of the connect from the new chief of Tyland Towers. She told him we were runnin' shit for the Emerald City Squad, which was common knowledge to most people, anyway. Stoney, the chief, ain't see nothing weird about givin' us the info when we told him we were running low and them niggas were in Vegas. The truth was, we gave away testers and put our own money together before we even approached him.

I was amazed at how cool, calm, and collected Yvette was about the whole matter. My girl was made for this life! Me? Well, I loved the glamour of it all, but I could've done without the violence. But Yvette, she proved over and over that she was *more* than willing to do whatever needed to be done to take over. I guess that's why I couldn't handle seeing her the way she was when Thick left her. It was like she was going through withdrawals. I couldn't help but wonder what was going on in her head now—even though she seemed to be doing the best out of all of us.

Carissa cried every time somebody in the hood asked her about Lavelle. She would break down the minute his name was called. And Kenyetta had been acting as if she didn't have time for us, outside of handling business. But it was cool, though. We all had to deal with shit the best way we could.

As for me, Cameron was my life, so I take my emotions out when I'm at home alone. Ain't no sense in me adding to the burdens. I'm tryin' to be strong for Yvette, because sometimes I feel like she's holdin' shit down by herself.

"Shit, girl! This nigga Dreyfus is paid for real!" Yvette said as she looked out the window at the four lush acres of land that his home sat on.

In the middle of his circular driveway was a huge waterfall. His place was laid. The huge yard was flanked by streams and bordered by a lush green forest. This was definitely different from what we're used to seeing, considering the only birds in the hood were pigeons.

"I guessed he would be livin' the life. Emerald City keeps his ass cozy with the price he charges on the weight."

"I know, I know. And that's why we need to stick to the plan," Yvette said as the butler immediately came to the car to greet us. "We're here for one purpose, and one purpose only, to convince him that business will be *better* with us than it was with them."

"How 'bout I just let you do the talkin', since you're more talented in the oral department than I am." I laughed.

"You heard that rumor too?" Yvette laughed while walking up his huge steps leading to his double doors. "Yeah . . . it's true. I do have skills. So let me handle this, little girl. You just watch my flow and take notes." She patted me on my back as she held the steel briefcase tightly in her hand.

Once inside, we were awestruck at the limestone floors, oak paneling, vaulted ceilings, and oversized fireplace. As with most drug kingpins, there were several beautiful women walking around, wearing tiny miniskirts. Some were carrying trays that held drinks and nose candy. The butler took us to the rotunda, where Dreyfus was drinking a glass of red wine. He looked much older and more reserved than I had envisioned him. If I saw him walking down the street, I would have pegged him for a senator instead of a kingpin. Looking up over the glasses resting on his nose, he stood up, shook our hands, and offered us seats.

The room had a fireplace tucked away in the corner. The crackling from the fire filled the air, considering he had yet to speak to us. His quiet nature put me on edge, and I wanted to grab Yvette's hand and run out the door. We had a nerve, thinkin' we could handle business on this level. The only thing that prevented me from running was the pencil-skirt suit I was wearing. It was so tight that I probably would've busted my ass tryin' to get out of there.

Yvette said we should rock the professional look, so we both had to run out and buy dress suits. We had a few fly-ass dresses in our closet, but nothing professional. I chose a white pencil-skirt suit, with the jacket buttoned all the way up, and no bra. My white pumps with the steel heel made the outfit classy but nasty. I turned shit out with my platinum necklace with the diamond drops.

Yvette was wearing a black formfitting suit, with a lace chemise under it. She looked vicious, showing off her thick, pretty legs.

"Now, what can I do for you, ladies?" he asked as he sipped from his wineglass.

"We're sorry to bother you, Dreyfus, but as you know, the fellas are away in Vegas, and Emerald City's low on supply," Yvette said.

"How is that? They just got over five hundred thousand dollars' worth of supply a few weeks ago. Are you telling me you're so low that you can't wait until they get back?"

"Yes, I am. I'm sure you know that we run Emerald City. All they do is stop by to check the status. So we're the best people to tell you what's going on. Which is why I wanted to discuss something else with you," Yvette said just as smoothly as the wind blows. "We aren't in business with them anymore. So if you want in on the Emerald City business, you'll be dealin' with us from now on."

Dreyfus's laughter pissed me off, but it didn't faze Yvette. She didn't smile and didn't take her eyes off his the entire time.

"And just how do you intend on running an operation *alone*? I mean, you are some very beautiful ladies, but I'm sure you know this business is a man's." He continued chuckling.

"I'm sorry, Dreyfus, we were under the impression your only concern was cash. Not whether it was dealt from a man or a woman," I said.

"It is!" he said angrily. "But be careful, pretty lady. Don't mistake my kindness for weakness.

219

Now, how do you know I'd even be interested in dealing with you? Man or woman?" he asked, turning his attention back to Yvette.

"Because we're here to settle *their* bill as well and to pay you up front for the weight we need now," Yvette said as she stood up and placed the steel suitcase on the table covering his newspaper. She popped open a suitcase containing over $500,000. Three hundred thousand was for the consignment, and the rest was for what we needed now. When the case was open, she turned it toward him.

"Well, I see you settled the bill, but there appears to be a little extra cash in here than what's owed," he said after seeing we were talking his language, Dollar Bill–ese. "So what's the deal?"

"Like I said, we're settling their bill and paying up front. I realize that in the past you worked on a consignment basis for Emerald City. Going forward, we're not going to operate like that. The interest we're paying is too high and the return is too low."

"Now, why should I accept money up front from you, when I can make almost thirty percent more on consignment with your little boyfriends?" He laughed. "This makes no fuckin' sense. You're not dealin' in the minor leagues. This is the majors!"

"You should accept our offer, because if you don't, you'll be cut out of the Emerald City profit altogether. Now, I know you've become accustomed to your glamorous lifestyle," Yvette said as she turned around as if seeing his place for the first time. "I mean, your place is phat. And I'm almost positive that Emerald City keeps you paid. I would hate to see you cut back a little," Yvette said slyly.

"You obviously didn't hear me, little girl!" Dreyfus yelled, becoming angry at the idea of a woman giving him options instead of the other way around. "Why the fuck should I fix somethin' that ain't broke? I'm fine with my current business arrangements. So unless you can tell me what *my* benefit is," he said as he removed stacks of money totaling $300,000 and closed the suitcase, "there ain't shit else to talk about."

"Did you know that the Emerald City Squad is in Vegas right now meeting a new connect?"

When my friend gave up that morsel of information, the smile was completely wiped off Dreyfus's face.

She continued her pitch. "When they return, they have plans to settle the bill and sever *all* the ties with you. We don't want to do that. We love the product you provide, and so do our customers. So what is your benefit? *Money,*" Yvette said, smiling. She knew from that point on, she had his full attention.

"We want to pay up front because we've had several attempts on the houses. We don't want unpaid product to be fucked with. We rather give you what's owed up front, and handle business on the side with whoever tries to fuck with us. We don't want the two connecting any-more," I said.

I could tell we had gotten to him, and that the news of possibly losing income in Emerald City wasn't sitting well with him.

"Uh . . . do you know this for sure?" he asked, more humble in his approach. "I can't see them telling you so much of their business."

"They have two women with them now in Vegas, and one of our lieutenants has a relation-ship with her. Well . . . an understanding, that is. And she advised him, and he told us," I said, try-ing to seal the deal that Yvette was closing. "So, do we have a commitment?"

"You can wait, if you'd like, until they return and tell you the same thing. But if you do that, our deal is no longer open to you," Yvette said.

Damn! My girl is going in for the kill.

Dreyfus took off his glasses and stood up. As he walked toward the door, we got a good glimpse at how tall he was. He had to be about six-three and was much more intimidating when standing. For a minute I thought he was getting ready to blast off our heads. Instead, he closed the door and locked it behind him; then he made his way over to the couch against the wall and took a seat. Then, as if he said something to Yvette, which I couldn't hear or understand, she stood up and removed her suit jacket, which revealed the curves of her breasts, hips, and legs. She slowly walked over to him and knelt down.

Finally figuring out what was going on, I stood up from my chair and removed my suit jacket as well. He smiled as he saw my bare breasts, with the diamond-dropped necklace in between them. Unzipping my skirt, I slid out of it, letting it fall to the floor, revealing my white lace panties and pumps.

I moved toward the couch, cradling him with my breasts against his face. Yvette had already brought him to stiffness. And for a man in his late forties, he had it going on in the dick department, for real. Tilting my head to the right so my soft curls could dress my shoulders and back, I kissed him on his lips, tasting a hint of the wine he had drunk just moments earlier. I hadn't noticed that Yvette had already slid out of her skirt, leaving nothing on but her black Jimmy Choo pumps and lace chemise. Working him to a complete thickness with her hand, she looked up at him and smiled at how his body shook as he anticipated her taking him into her mouth.

"Dreyfus," she started to say in a low, soft voice, "do we have a deal?"

"Yes. . . ." He moaned as she engulfed him fully, while I fed him my nipples. "We have a deal," he managed to say.

I was surprised at the tongue skills he possessed on my breasts. I knew this was business, but I had all intentions of taking advantage. Plus he was paid, and power always turned me on. He impressed me so much with his tongue action that I was able to rearrange the setup to my advantage.

Yvette continued to suck his dick, while I positioned my ass directly over his face. His pussy-eating skills were as good as I'd hoped they'd be. He grabbed my ass while his tongue searched ferociously around my pussy, devouring up all the months of built-up tension. I was on the verge of cumming when I tried to pull away to give my girl enough time to do what she was doing. But as if he were a starving man, he placed his hands on my lower back, pulling me closer toward his face. I had no other choice but to explode inside the mouth of a business associate, a man I really didn't know. When I turned, I saw Yvette was already done and dressed.

I got off him and quickly got dressed too. Yvette walked to his desk and wrote down her number. He smiled at both of us and wiped my wetness off his mouth with a napkin. Tying his robe tightly, and putting his glasses back on, he told us when and where the weight would be delivered and to arrange for someone to unload it. We were almost out the door when he called us back.

"Ladies."

"Yes?" Yvette said, holding the empty suitcase in her hand.

"I wasn't implying for you to go that far. I was sold the moment you told me they were using a new connect."

"I know," Yvette said, smiling.

"And you did it, anyway?" he asked.

"Yeah . . . I was tryin' to show you there are several benefits to working with women. And today you learned one of the most lucrative. Good night, Dreyfus. We'll be in contact," she said as we walked out the door.

"You's a bad bitch!" I laughed. "Do you even have a heart?" I continued to comment as we jumped into my Mercedes, which the valet had pulled around front for us.

"Not anymore. Not anymore."

Chapter 28

The Time Is Now

February, Friday, 8:10 P.M.

Derrick

The gatekeepers called a meeting in the community center around the back of the Emerald City projects.

The meeting consisted of Doctanian, Derrick, Bruce, Jones, Harold, and Ed. They called the meeting to let everybody know what was going on from here on out. Some people were happy about the change, because they didn't care for the Emerald City Squad. Others weren't pleased.

"So what are we supposed to do when they ask us what's up with their cash?" Harold asked as he sat in his chair, balancing himself on the back two legs. "This doesn't make any sense."

"You're supposed to tell them to see us about

it," Yvette responded, looking him dead in the eyes. "You can put full responsibility on us."

"You sure 'bout that." He laughed as he looked at Ed.

"I'm positive," she snapped. "But can you handle what we're asking you to do?"

"Hey . . . as long as I get my cash, I ain't trippin'." He laughed as he gave Ed a dap.

"So why you ask?" Yvette shot back, not liking his response.

"Huh?" Harold said.

"I said, if you were totally comfortable, all of that shit you asked me before was a waste of fuckin' time," she said, making him feel stupid.

"Does anybody else have any *legitimate* questions?" Mercedes added, in an attempt to help Yvette gain control over the meeting.

"I do," Derrick said, sizing Mercedes up in her black fitted pants and black button-down top.

"Go ahead, Derrick," Mercedes said.

"Are y'all good on manpower? I can give up two more of my boys, if the ones you have on my squad ain't enough."

"Naw, we good. Thanks," she said, giving him a look that lingered on longer than it should have. It was clear that they were feeling each other.

"Well, if nobody else has any other questions, the meeting is adjourned. I'm expectin' them to come through tomorrow night. Be on guard. If you see anything suspicious, hit us on the BlackBerry," Yvette added.

As the lieutenants made their way to the door, Yvette called Doctanian and Derrick back. When she was sure the others were out of sight, she addressed them.

"Listen . . . I'm gonna need y'all to be lookin' out for Harold and Ed. I have a feelin' they gonna do us greasy," Yvette whispered.

"I was thinkin' the same thing," Derrick said.

"And you know whatever I can do, I'm in," Doctanian added.

"Thanks. Have you heard anything 'bout Jordan yet?" Mercedes asked Doctanian.

Everything about him had changed since Jordan had gone missing. He didn't take care of his appearance the way he used to. He let himself go and wasn't sociable. The biggest indicator that he wasn't the same came from Li'l C. He kept coming to her saying something was wrong with Doctanian. Mercedes was afraid her son had gotten attached to a man who owed him nothing. It was also the first time she'd ever seen her son worried.

"No, I ain't heard nothin'. I'm tellin' you, if somebody hurt her, I'ma kill 'em!" he said, fighting back tears.

"I understand. And if *you* need us to do anything, let me know."

"And if I hear anything, I'm puttin' it to anybody who got anything to do with it!" Derrick said. "That's my word."

"Thanks, man! She's pregnant wit' my kid!" he said, forcing back tears.

Yvette and Mercedes liked Doctanian. He was a real man who was true to the game, and he didn't deserve the hand he was being dealt. But at the same time, they had a business to run. The quandary now was: Did they keep him on and jeopardize the organization? Or fire him, which would ultimately be a slap in his face?

"Take it easy, Doctanian. We'll talk to you later," Yvette said.

"Thanks." He walked out the door.

After he walked away, the three of them were left alone.

"Derrick, keep an eye on him. I'm worried," Yvette said.

"Done," Derrick said.

Chapter 29

Somethin' Ain't Right

February, Monday, 7:10 P.M.

Thick

"I'm telling you, them bitches are up to somethin'! Why can't we get through to nobody at EC?" Thick yelled as he drove to Emerald City.

"Calm down, man. Sometimes you blow shit outta proportion!" Cam wasn't feeling how Thick was acting anymore. The truth was, the stunt Thick had pulled in the hotel—bringing them the girls and then keeping them in his own room the whole time—pissed Cameron off. It wasn't because he liked the girls or anything, but it was the principle. Thick didn't even ask Cam if he could slide off with the shortie who was supposed to be for him. That's just the type of grimy-ass nigga Thick had become.

"Yeah, man, you wildin' out now. We on our

way now. We'll see what the deal is," Lavelle added. "No need to get worked up yet."

"I know one thing, if Yvette fuckin' wit' me, I'm puttin' my hands around her throat."

While on the way to EC, Cam's cell phone rang. He smiled when he saw it was Li'l C's number. He hadn't spoken to his son since he returned from Vegas. He missed him and his mother, but Cam couldn't express how much he missed her. He had to keep it real with Li'l C about his and Mercedes' relationship, and right now they were over.

"Hey, man!" Cam yelled into the phone.

"Hey, Dad." Li'l C wasn't his usual upbeat self. "When I'm seein' you?"

"Damn, man," Cam responded. "Everything a'ight? You sound a little out of it."

"Not really."

Thick started blasting the music in the truck. Cam was trying to talk to his son and Thick was acting stupid. Cam had to be careful in his approach. Number one, it was wrong to tell a man to adjust the volume in his own truck; and number two, Thick was a hot head. Saying the wrong thing could almost guarantee an argument, but Thick was going to turn the music down— whether he wanted to or not.

"Hey, man, you mind turnin' that shit down?" Cam asked.

"Actually, I do."

Lavelle and Dyson were pissed about his response. Li'l C was like their nephew, and they couldn't believe how Thick was acting.

"Come on, man. Turn that shit down so the man can talk to his son!" Lavelle yelled over the music.

Thick looked at Cameron through the mirror, and Cam stared him dead in the eyes.

"Aw, come on. Cam don't know when a nigga playin' wit' him?" Thick joked as he adjusted the volume. "Y'all niggas been blowin' me all weekend, actin' all serious and shit. Tell Li'l C, I said what up."

Cameron ignored him. He couldn't believe how Thick had been acting ever since Dex was killed. Cam couldn't stand him, and he was starting to even hate Thick.

"Dad . . . is everything okay?" Li'l C questioned.

For a second Cam was so caught up in his anger that he didn't hear his son.

"Dad. You there?"

"Oh . . . yeah. I didn't hear you at first, li'l man. But what's goin' on with you?"

"They can't find Jordan . . . and Doc don't hang wit' me no more. It's like he don't even know me."

Cam was listening to his son, but he also peeped how Thick kept eyeing him through the rearview mirror. He wondered what was up with that.

"What you mean, they can't find Jordan?" Cam didn't know a lot about her, but he did know she was Doctanian's girl.

"They don't know where she at. Momma says they been lookin', but I think somebody got her."

"Don't worry about stuff like that, Li'l C. Leave the worryin' to me."

"Okay."

"Where you at?" Cam asked, positive that more drama was going on in Emerald City than he thought.

"I'm at Cousin Vickie's in Virginia."

"Cousin Vickie's? Is Chante and the baby wit' you too?" Cam knew it was weird for them to be over there, because Mercedes couldn't stand Vickie. She knew Vickie would do right by the kids, but this was very strange. Knowing just how much Mercedes hated Vickie's guts, he couldn't help but wonder how she ended up smoothing things out enough to drop their children off with her.

"Yep. We all over here. She says we gonna be here till it all blows over."

"Till what blows over?" Cam asked, wondering how much Li'l C really knew.

"She calls it 'the showdown.' "

Cam was quiet. *The Showdown?* he thought. *What in the fuck is this bitch up to?*

"Listen, Li'l C," he said. "Doc will be okay. I'll holla at him when I get back to EC."

234

"For real? That's what's up!"

"Yeah, don't worry about it."

"He said we were gonna start a music company together. He said if I stopped selling drugs, we'd be like Dame Dash and Jay-Z!"

"What?" Cam yelled, taking in what he had just heard. He yelled so loud that everybody turned around to ear hustle in on what he was saying to Li'l C. "What you talkin' 'bout, man? What do you mean, he stopped you from selling drugs!"

"Yeah." Li'l C hesitated. "It's okay now. I'm not doin' it anymore."

Cam was listening, but all he was thinking about was which one of them niggas put him on. He knew it was just a matter of time before Li'l C got into the life, but he imagined it would be when his son was older.

I'm gonna kill whoever the fuck disrespected me! That's my word! Cam thought.

"You all right, man?" Thick asked.

"I'm good."

"Li'l C," Cam said real low. "Who gave you weight to sell? And tell me the truth."

Li'l C paused. "Uncle Thick did."

Chapter 30

Too Little, Too Late

February, Monday, 9:30 P.M.

Doctanian

"Are you sure? Don't play wit' me!" Doctanian told one of the heads.

"Yeah, I'm sure. I saw him meet her round back and then dump her body later," he said, anticipating the reward Doctanian would give him for the news.

Doctanian's body was shaking with anger. He couldn't believe he'd lost the love of his life at the hands of his most trusted soldier.

"Doc! Look at your leg!"

When he looked down, he saw piss streaming down the jeans that he'd worn for the past few days. Ever since he'd been trying to find Jordan, he'd been an emotional wreck. He didn't take care of his body. He didn't eat. And most of all, he didn't care for anything or anybody.

Without saying a word, he walked off. He was too angry to be embarrassed that he was walking in his own piss. He hadn't had an episode like that since he was a kid. When he was younger, whenever he was afraid or upset, he would piss in his bed. It went on for years because his father would beat his mother and he'd stay awake at night, feeling defenseless and helpless. It didn't stop until he and his mother moved to Emerald City together.

"Hey!" the dope fiend yelled. "What 'bout my stuff?"

Doctanian turned around and the fiend rushed over to him. Doctanian handed him everything he had in his pockets.

Doctanian was sure the fiend would spend all night getting high, and Doctanian didn't care.

Because in his mind Doctanian felt tonight would be his last night alive.

Chapter 31

Holla at You

February, Monday, 9:40 P.M.

Doctanian

"Let me holla at you for a second, man," Doctanian said with a glazed look in his eye.

"Naw, Joe. I got somewhere to go right now," Erick responded, holding on to the weapon in his pocket.

Erick wasn't a fool. He saw the crazed look in the other man's eyes and he knew what the deal was. Doctanian had been walking around like a mummy ever since Erick dumped Jordan's lifeless body into a Dumpster.

"Why, man? Any other time you got conversation for me. Why not now?"

They were in the same alley where CJ and Charles had been killed. Their bodies were pumping adrenaline as they realized that somebody wouldn't be leaving the alley alive.

"She was a whore! I had to do it," Erick said, feeling there was no need in wasting time or lying. He decided to get the shit out in the open. "You gonna end what we got over a whore? Think about what we could have, man. Let's take down these bitches and make shit happen! I talked to Ed and Harold and they ready to take them bitches out tonight! What's up? Let's put this shit to the side, man!"

Tears rolled down his face as he focused on Erick. Doctanian knew Erick was only talking to throw him off. The moment he let his guard down, Erick's gun would be in his back.

"Why you hurt Jordan? You knew she was all I had," Doctanian asked, searching for answers that he knew Erick didn't have.

"Are you serious?" Erick laughed, taking his gun out of his pocket. "I'm telling you, we got a chance at a dynasty, and you worried about a bitch and a baby that probably wasn't even yours?" Erick laughed. "Are you really that soft?"

His words stabbed him in the heart.

"Are you telling me you fucked my girl?" He took two steps toward him.

"That's exactly what I'm saying. And I fucked her well."

With that, Doctanian took his gun out and, without the slightest hesitation, pulled the trigger. But as if he were a character in a bad movie, nothing came out.

"Oh snap! This really is my lucky day!" Erick

laughed, relieved he wasn't shot. "But it ain't yours," he said.

Erick aimed his weapon, but he dropped to his knees before he could get off a shot. Doctanian watched in amazement as a round of bullets found a home inside his back. His knees hit the ground first as he looked at Doctanian, and then he fell to the concrete, facedown, revealing who was behind him.

Derrick had kept his promise to the girls and looked after Doctanian, after all.

Instead of feeling relief, Doctanian ran to pick up Erick's gun and placed it in his mouth. Derrick rushed him, taking it away.

"What in the fuck is wrong wit' you, man? Why you doin' this?"

"Cuz I don't deserve to live!" he cried.

"Come on, man! He's dead. We killed his ass for Jordan."

"No . . . I don't deserve to live, because it was my fault Jordan was murdered."

"Why you say that?" Derrick asked.

"Because he was punishing me for killing Stacia and Dex."

Chapter 32

Get at Me

February, Monday, 10:15 P.M.

Thick

"Hey, man, open the gate! What the fuck you waitin' on?" Thick yelled.

"I'm sorry, Thick. I have to phone Yvette first."

"The fuck you mean, you have to phone Yvette!"

Thick was growing irritated at the way the guard was treating him. In the past the moment any of the guards saw his truck, they'd fling open the gate to Emerald City. But here a guard was, acting as if Thick was a customer and didn't deserve the VIP treatment he was accustomed to.

"Y'all hear this shit, man?" he asked as he looked back at Cameron and the others. "Them bitches really askin' for it! This is what the fuck I was talkin' about."

"Well, we're here now," Cameron responded,

still salty at what Li'l C had told him about Thick giving him dope to sell. "We'll see what's up."

When the time was right, Cameron would step to Thick about the situation.

Lavelle and Dyson were quiet as they waited on the word from the guard. They were mentally preparing for what they would have to do, and what they knew Thick wanted to do. There wasn't a doubt in any of their minds that tonight, somebody would die.

It was just a matter of who it would be.

"Okay, sir!" the guard said. "You can go through now." The gate rose.

"The next time you see me . . . you gonna wish you didn't pull this shit," Thick promised. "Don't let them bitches fill your head. I run . . . I mean, we run shit in Emerald City," he corrected himself, realizing his own selfish motives almost slipped out.

The guard didn't say anything. He knew he had to stick to the orders Yvette and the other women had given him. They treated him better than Thick ever had.

Pulling up in front of Unit C, they noticed the women weren't on post. Thick got cocky when he saw that. He immediately started thinking that they must've been frightened after the shit they pulled at the gate and were hiding out. But the others knew better. They realized something more was going on, and everything was changing tonight.

"Derrick . . . get down here!" Thick yelled as they all jumped out of the truck.

Derrick moved slowly. He no longer showed urgency, the way they were used to seeing. Thick, Cameron, Lavelle, and Dyson noticed that their authority had been diminished.

"Yeah . . . what you need?" Derrick asked nonchalantly.

"What I need? What I need? Who the fuck you talkin' to like that, nigga?" Thick shot back as he walked up on Derrick. "You got a death wish, son?"

Derrick took two steps back, brushed off his coat, and said, "Like I said . . . what you need?"

When Cameron saw Thick was getting ready to pull his gun out of his coat and kill Derrick, he stepped up to him. Five of Derrick's soldiers hurried to Derrick's side. When Lavelle and Dyson saw that, they all rushed to Thick's side too. Right or wrong, they weren't tolerating disrespect from somebody who was under them.

"I know you ain't crazy, D!" Lavelle said. "So you betta start telling us, what the fuck is up?"

"I asked a question, and I still ain't got an answer to it. What do y'all need?" Derrick was unmoved by them. "Y'all here to cop some dope or what?" His soldiers were on point to blast the squad's heads off; and if they missed, they had ten other soldiers hidden from view with sniper weapons ready to snub them out.

Thick was struck motionless and speechless.

In all his life he always had provoked fear, but tonight was different.

"Where Yvette and them?" Dyson asked, taking control of the situation.

"I'll take y'all to 'em," Derrick said.

"Yeah . . . we need to find out what the fuck is goin' on round here," Cameron demanded.

While the others talked, Thick's eyes stayed glued on Derrick. Any other day he would've killed him where he stood, but this time was different. He was walking into a situation blind, and he wanted to be cool and get some answers first. But he also wanted Derrick to know that he wouldn't forget his disrespect and would be handling him later.

Derrick, sensing the hate in Thick's eyes, said, "I feel the same way, playa."

Silence.

"Yo, Doc . . . come around and pick us up around front. We takin' Thick and them to the girls," Derrick said into his walkie-talkie.

"You got it, man."

When Thick heard Doctanian's voice, Thick developed a plan.

Doctanian pulled up in a White Ford Excursion five minutes later. Derrick jumped into the passenger seat, and the other soldiers hopped into the back. Before they pulled off, Thick asked to speak to Doc in private.

"You want us to go with you?" Lavelle asked.

"Naw . . . go wait in the truck."

Doc hopped out of the driver's seat and they walked together. Thick was going to do his best to play on his emotions. But what Thick didn't know was that Jordan was already dead, so Doctanian didn't have anything or anybody else to lose.

"Listen . . . I need you to do me a favor," Thick said to Doctanian with his hand on his back. His mouth was hidden from view so that no one could read his lips but Doc.

"And what's that?"

"I need you to take out Derrick, and possibly Yvette and them bitches."

Doctanian turned to him and said, "Sorry, youngin' . . . I can't do nothin' for you."

Thick couldn't believe what was going on. He was the most ruthless out of the group, and everyone was carrying the utmost fuck out of him tonight.

What are these bitches doin'? Fuckin' these dudes? he thought.

"Oh, for real? I wonder if you would feel the same way if I paid a little visit to your girl," Thick threatened.

Doctanian wasn't moved. He had already lost Jordan, and Yvette and the girls were the only family he had. It was through blackmail that Thick had been able to get him to kill Dex and Stacia. Thick told him he would gut out his pregnant girlfriend and maybe even his mother. So, with no more convincing needed, Doc did what he was told. The look in Dex's and Stacia's eyes still fucked with him till this day. Instead of being scared when he popped up out of nowhere requesting a ride to the ball, they smiled—not knowing that he was there to kill them. But it was Thick who decided to slice their bodies, and Doctanian hated him for that. Almost as much as he hated not being man enough to stand up to Thick. But tonight all of that had changed.

Telling everything to Derrick lifted a major weight off his shoulders. He didn't even tell Jordan about his hand in Stacia's and Dex's murders because he didn't want to get her involved.

"I don't know what she'll say, man. . . . She's dead," he said as he walked back to the truck and jumped in, leaving Thick standing alone, looking stupid.

"You comin' or not?" Doctanian asked from the driver's side of the truck.

Thick decided to bite his words, but now he had added Doctanian to his list, along with Doc's mother. And since Doctanian liked Li'l C so much, he was gonna take him out too.

Thick jumped into his truck and pulled up alongside theirs.

"Where we goin'?"

"To the community center," Derrick said as Doctanian started the truck. "Follow us."

"Hold up right quick," Thick said when his phone vibrated.

He was shocked to see who it was. Yvette was

calling him. He laughed; and before he answered, he showed the squad members the caller ID.

"You can't be serious!" Lavelle said.

"Answer it," Cameron added. "Maybe we can find out what the fuck is going on."

"Hello."

"Thick . . . I see you out front. Why don't you come upstairs and talk to me for a second," Yvette said, sounding as if they were still together. "I got something I want to give to you."

"Oh really?" He laughed.

"Yes . . . and your key still works," she said as she hung up.

When Thick hung up as well, he noticed Derrick and the others still looking at him.

"You rollin' or what, man?" Derrick asked.

"Naw . . . Cameron and them going. I got something else to take care of now."

He told his friends that Yvette wanted to see him and that he may have to choke her.

"You sure you don't want us comin' with you?" Lavelle asked. "This seems like a setup."

"Nigga, please. I'm time enough for a bitch. She not crazy enough to fuck wit' me," he said, jumping out of the truck. "You drive, Cam!"

Cameron got in the front seat. Thick waved them off and went into the building.

He had one thing on his mind: putting Yvette in her place.

Chapter 33

Full Circle

February, Monday, 10:45 P.M.

Thick

Walking up to the door felt eerie to Thick.

However, being the arrogant, cocky man he was, he pushed his feelings to the side and walked into the apartment that he had once shared with Yvette, acting as though they still lived there . . . *together.* What he saw next, he couldn't deny. Everything in the apartment was gone. It looked the same as it had when they first moved in.

With the door still open, and his hand tucked in his coat for his piece, he walked in. With the door slightly ajar, he used the light in the hallway to help him see. The only things in the apartment were two chairs in the middle of the floor. He tried to flip the switch for the lights, but they didn't come on. He saw Yvette sitting in one of the chairs as she lit two candles.

Thick flipped the switch again, as if flipping it the first ten times had been a fluke.

"Thick . . . it's not on. Come in and have a seat."

The chair Yvette was sitting in was directly across from the empty one. When Thick closed the door, the light from the candle revealed her sexy, small frame. He couldn't help but admire how good she looked. She was wearing all black and had her hair combed down her back. The tight black pants she had on made her legs look even more appealing. The button-down shirt she had on kissed her cleavage perfectly as the diamonds she had in her earrings and on her neck illuminated the way.

Thick walked in and took his seat. The candle in between the chairs cast a glow on both their faces.

"What's up, Yvette? I'm here. You got somebody in here for me or somethin'? 'Cause if you do, bring it on."

"Nobody's here, Thick."

He went through the apartment to inspect himself and found she was telling the truth.

"You see?" Yvette smiled. "It's just you and me."

Her glossy lips answered his questions elegantly. Yvette didn't appear nervous, and her mannerisms put Thick on edge.

"Well, what the fuck is up then?" he asked, taking his seat again.

"You were always a man who liked to get to the point."

"Yep . . . and shit ain't changed, so stop wasting my muthafuckin' time!"

"Shit ain't changed, Thick?" She laughed. "Shit ain't changed? A lot of shit has changed."

"Oh yeah . . . like what?"

"For starters, you ruined my life and left me to pick up the pieces by myself."

"Is that what this is about?" He laughed again. His deep voice rocked the empty apartment. "Damn bitch! I thought you'd be over Big T by now."

"I wanna know why?" She was unmoved by his comments.

"Why I do what? Stop fuckin' wit' you?"

"Yes."

"Cuz you're weak! That's why."

"I hold shit down for you and you call me weak? I wonder how many other women could hold shit down for their men."

"You probably right. But you wanted to do it. That's why it was so easy for you to hold shit down."

"Is that what you think, Thick?" She crossed her legs. "Do you really believe I wanted to be a hustler, riskin' my life every day?"

"I know you did."

"Well, you're wrong. I wanted you, but you chose another bitch over me. You gave her my life and left me wit' nothin'. I would've done anything for you, Thick. Anything you asked me."

"I know. That's the problem." He laughed. "You didn't have limits, and she wasn't that way. Plus she took a scar for me."

"So she gets in a car accident . . . and gets a scar on her face, and then wins points with you? Are you serious?"

"Yeah . . . I am."

When he said that, Yvette reached under her leg and pulled out a pearl-handled knife. Thick sat up in his seat and pulled out his gun.

"She gets a scar and you chose her, huh?" With that said, she took the knife and sliced along her jawline. As the blood trickled down, she never took her eyes off his. "I bet you, she wouldn't have done that shit."

Thick looked at her and suddenly he was turned on. Yvette was more thorough than he had thought. She reminded him of the old Yvette he dated, but better.

"You a crazy bitch. But I like that shit!"

"I'm glad you do. Now . . . on to business. Your services are no longer needed in Emerald City. We're takin' over."

"Fuck you talkin' 'bout, Yvette? You sound stupid!" His voice boomed through the empty apartment.

She sat firm in her chair, not fazed at all. "I'm talkin' 'bout how you gonna die tonight."

Thick wasn't laughing anymore. He thought after she cut her face, she'd beg to be back with him. But here she was, threatening to kill him!

"Yeah, okay. And just how you supposed to do that?"

"Like this," she said as she pitched the knife through the air, burying it into his neck.

She stood up and walked toward him. The same slick, manipulative eyes she'd become accustomed to were two sizes larger than usual. He tried desperately to get the knife out of his neck, but he couldn't move.

Standing behind him, she whispered in his ear, "You see, baby. Some promises you gotta keep."

When his big body slid out of the chair and onto the floor, she grabbed her coat and moved toward the door.

Chapter 34

A Room

February, Monday, 10:55 P.M.

Yvette

I did what the fuck I had to do!

I gave him my life. My fucking life! And what did he do, he acted like he couldn't remember it. Killing him was as easy as getting my pussy ate. That's right . . . it felt so good, I could've cum. I didn't choose this life; it chose me. And I accepted it . . . for him.

When I opened up the door to the community center, I was happy to see Cameron, Lavelle, and Dyson were there. Kenyetta, Carissa, and Mercedes were there also. I could tell by the look in the men's eyes that they were scared when I appeared without Thick.

My girls were wondering what had happened to my face, so I motioned to them with my eyes that everything was okay.

"Hello, gentlemen," I said, not explaining Thick's absence or my fresh scar. "How are you doin' tonight?"

"Stop playin' games, Yvette. What the fuck is goin' on?" Lavelle asked.

"Please . . . have a seat," I told them.

As they took their seats around the table in the community center's meeting room, I was trying to be careful. I had a big decision to make tonight. A person might have thought that the biggest decision I had to make was killing Thick. But that was easy and necessary. He would've never relinquished Emerald City to us.

When they all had a seat, and Derrick, Doctanian, and the other soldiers remained standing, surrounding the table, I sat down across from them. Mercedes, Kenyetta, and Carissa sat down next to me. I could see the love they had for them, but I could also feel the loyalty they had to me. Besides, we all had been lied to and betrayed; as far as I was concerned, we were no longer loyal to them.

"I'm not gonna beat round the bush wit' you. . . . We takin' over Emerald City," I said, looking into all of their eyes.

"This bitch is delusional!" Cameron laughed. "How the fuck you gonna run Emerald City alone?"

"Easy," Mercedes answered. "Have you forgotten who's been runnin' shit, anyway?"

"You've been runnin' shit wit' our help," Lavelle responded.

"Actually, I don't think we'll notice the difference. You haven't had our backs in a while," Carissa said.

"First off . . . you don't have a relationship with Dreyfus. He don't fuck wit' females like that, so your supply would be cut the fuck off," Dyson added.

We all started laughing, makin' them even more anxious. After all, we were telling them how their futures would turn out, and there wasn't a damn thing they could do about it.

"Yeah . . . Dreyfus is somethin' else, isn't he?" I said.

"Yes, he is . . . and he doesn't work wit' females," Cameron added.

"Maybe . . . maybe not," I told him. "All I know is he has a badass house. I'm telling you, the waterfall was outrageous. What did you think, Mercedes?"

"I don't know, Yvette," she said as she shrugged her shoulders. "I liked his head better. He can suck a mean pussy."

Cameron's face went red out of anger. "Oh, so you fuckin' Dreyfus now?"

"Sit down, playa," Derrick said. "Slow your roll."

Cameron looked up at him and sat back down.

"And where are my fucking kids while you out tossing pussy at that nigga? Huh? Where my kids?"

Mercedes laughed. "Don't worry, baby. . . . They weren't there."

Cameron wanted to smack the shit out of Mercedes, but Lavelle pulled him back down.

"What makes you think we'd just walk away from a million-dollar empire?"

"For one, we've doubled the salary of our soldiers, so they have our backs, and Dreyfus doesn't want to fuck wit' you for your betrayal in Vegas," I told them.

"Y'all told him about that?" Dyson asked.

"Of course!" Kenyetta laughed.

"And how did y'all know?" Cameron added.

"Let's just say, y'all should choose the female company y'all take with you on business trips more wisely in the future," I advised.

Lavelle shook his head in disgust.

"So y'all have a connection wit' Dreyfus and now we're out, huh? Well, what about the money we put in this shit? We ain't walkin' away empty-handed," Dyson said.

With that, I snapped my fingers; one of the soldiers placed a steel suitcase on the table. I popped the latches, looked at the money, and turned it around to them.

"It's all there," I assured them, sliding the case across the table.

They looked at each other, visibly shook.

"Well, what'll happen if we don't buy this shit?" Cameron inquired.

"Then you'll end up like Thick," I said.

"And how's that?" Lavelle asked.

I looked around the table. "Dead."

They jumped up from their seats and pulled out weapons as our soldiers placed three barrels to their heads apiece.

"Don't make this nastier than it has to be. You did us wrong, and you know it. Now it's time to step down," I said. "Either way somebody loses, but don't forget about the kids involved. If you don't step down, somebody will get killed, because we won't stop fighting until the last breath leaves our bodies. And that could mean Li'l C without a mother or father. Or what about Lavelle's kids? Everybody loses if these guns pop in here tonight."

"Y'all have other shops. Y'all don't need EC," Carissa said.

The looks on their faces were ones of defeat, remorse, and guilt. They knew they had done us wrong and we deserved Emerald City. No fuck that, we earned it! They also knew if they didn't step down, we were fully prepared for war.

"So what's up? Do you step down or not?" I said.

They looked at each other and grabbed the money off the table without saying a word.

"That was a good decision," Yvette said. "Now, can you do us one more solid?"

"And what the fuck is that, Yvette?" Cameron

responded, still not believing everything that had taken place.

"Take your dead friend with you. He's up in my apartment."

Chapter 35
The Confrontation
February, Monday, 11:05 P.M.

Emerald City

Cameron and the other, old EC Squad were twisted up a little about how things had gone down.

Part of them wanted to do more, but the girls' soldiers had them outnumbered. It was obvious that any of these men would've given their lives for the girls, no questions asked.

Cameron, Lavelle, and Dyson eased into Yvette's apartment. They were met by the smell of blood and fear as soon as they opened the door. However, it wasn't the smell of death floating in the air that made them grab for their weapons. It was the movement.

"Help . . . me," Thick said, barely above a whisper. "Help . . . me."

They all rushed to his side, with the light from the candle leading them.

"We thought you were dead, man!" Lavelle yelled.

"We'll get you out of here," Dyson added.

They were helpful, but Cameron wasn't.

The thought of all of the trouble Thick had caused consumed him. All of this shit was Thick's greedy-ass fault. Had Thick not brought Zakayla into the picture, Cam would be marrying Mercedes, and business would have been as usual.

He looked at Dyson and Lavelle.

As if they could read his mind, Dyson said, "Make it quick."

"We'll be in the hallway," Lavelle added, taking one last look at Thick, the man he once called a friend.

Cameron stooped down in front of Thick, who was moving on the floor, trying to hang on to life.

"Help me. Please."

"I want my face to be the last face you see."

"Cam . . . get me outta here," he begged. "I'm dying, nigga!"

"I'm sorry, dawg. I can't do shit for you."

Thick dragged his bloody body along the floor and tried to appeal to Cameron.

"Why, man? Why? Why are you doing this to me?"

"Because you fucked with the wrong nigga's

son," Cameron said as he placed his gun to Thick's head. "And now you know."

He pulled his trigger and blasted the bullet into Thick's skull. Once the shot was heard, Lavelle and Dyson came back into the apartment.

"Well . . . let's get rid of this muthafucka," Lavelle said.

"Yeah, let's get rid of him."

Epilogue

Two years later . . .

Life in Emerald City was different.

The gatekeepers didn't have to hold down the gate anymore. They all moved back to the steps of Emerald City, three times out of the week, and empowered their soldiers to do the work. They made decisions to enjoy life with the people who meant the most—their families and each other.

Mercedes got with Derrick and had another baby. They bought a house in Upper Marlboro, Maryland. Derrick was still holding shit down in Emerald City with his crew. He realized that reporting to a woman wasn't as bad as he thought.

Carissa got back with Lavelle, but she tried to do it on the DL. She would sneak off to see him.

When Yvette let on that she knew, Carissa said she feared that they would reject her. Because they all knew that Lavelle really loved her, no matter what, they agreed the two at least deserved a chance.

Kenyetta started keeping time with one of the Tyland Towers dudes. Nobody knew who he was, and nobody asked too many questions either. She said that when he was worth introducing, she'd bring him around, but not a minute sooner.

Yvette didn't mess with anybody anymore. Everybody swore she was keeping time with a female—some chick named Spinner—but she denied it. The more she denied it, the more they felt she was lying up with her. But just like they accepted Carissa and Lavelle, they would accept Yvette—because no matter what, they loved her.

Cameron had a hard time letting Mercedes go. He did everything—from coming by her and Derrick's house at all hours of the night, asking about the whereabouts of his kids, to showing up at places they were and starting trouble. When none of that worked, he finally confessed his love to Mercedes, but she said she was in love with Derrick. And when he saw it in her eyes, he left it alone.

One of Dyson's soldiers at one of his shops outside of Emerald robbed and killed him. His body was never found; and to this day Cameron and the crew are looking for whoever killed him.

Doctanian left the game and opened a sports bar. He moved his mother out of the projects and kept money stashed to keep his promise to Li'l C about starting their video production company. He had a baby with a girl he met at his bar and was very happy.

Emerald City was built on fear and run by lies, but it was uplifted by fearless women, who weren't afraid to call out the men in their lives.

And although their men broke their promises, the women were better for it.

Fuck a happily-ever-after ending! This a muthafuckin' hood tale! Now let me show you how shit really went down.

Chapter 36

Now the Drama Really Begins

December 13, Monday, 9:33 P.M.

Cameron

Cameron sat outside in his black BMW 750i without the heat running in the car.

It was thirty degrees outside and the wind was mighty. Despite the weather, his body was pumping fire due to what he was about to do. As hard as he tried, he couldn't get over losing Mercedes—despite the breakup being all his fault. He felt betrayed, and it caused him to mastermind the ultimate plan. When he saw Black Water walk toward his car, he hit the automatic unlock button. Black Water opened the car door and climbed in the passenger seat. He was wearing a thick red North Face coat.

They called him Black Water because his complexion was dark; and whether it was cold or hot outside, his skin kept its oily luster. Snow from the outside fell onto the butter-colored leather seat. His build was as large as Thick's had been. In a way he reminded Cameron of him. That was another reason why he had trouble trusting him, but he pushed the thought out of his mind because he was blinded by fury.

"Why you ain't got the heat on, man? It's cold as shit in here!" Black Water said, reaching over and hitting the button, releasing a soft blast of warm air into the car.

Cameron mugged him, wanting to give him a piece of his mind for touching the controls in his car. The only reason he didn't was because he needed his help. Black Water had a lot of power in Tyland Towers, so he'd come in handy for what he wanted done.

"I ain't ask you out here to make you comfortable. This is about business," Cameron said, his eyes hidden under the black New York Yankees cap he wore.

"So what *do* you want?"

"I want you to help me get Emerald back," Cameron said coldly.

"Get Emerald back?" Black Water chuckled. "I heard you niggas handed it over. Why you want it back now?"

The fact that everyone talked about how the

Emerald City Squad stepped down for some women bugged the hell out of him.

"Yeah, well, you shouldn't believe everything you hear. I was gettin' enough money to keep me tight, but now I want more." He was lying. Cameron was still well-off with his shops in and around D.C. His real reason for the scheming betrayal of his children's mother was jealousy— pure and simple.

"You got people who can help me get in? I hear them shorties got that thing on lock over there."

"Yeah. My men Harold and Ed still there, and they waitin' on my word. You shouldn't have a problem breakin' shit down, wit' my help. We just gonna have to be slow and careful."

"Cool," he said, satisfied with his response. "So when you wanna start?"

"Today."

"And what about her?"

Cameron was silent. He knew that once he gave the word, he couldn't change his mind later. He had to be clear about his intention for Mercedes.

"Kill her."

Everyone's got a "hate list"—but in this explicit street tale, one woman plans to do something about it. . . .

Don't miss Reign's

Hate List: Be Careful Who You Cross

On sale now from Dafina Books

1

Hood Love at Its Best

The summer air was hypnotic, and a perfect breeze was blowing through and around the inner-city buildings that night. Nineteen-year-old Yvonna's red Prada stilettos clicked quickly against the concrete pavement, which led toward her block.

She was irritated that the gum she was chewing had lost its flavor and that the thong she was wearing had run so far up her ass, it was difficult to walk. She would've freed herself from the uncomfortable feeling, but she was almost at her building in Southeast D.C. Not to mention her hands were occupied with grocery bags filled with food.

"You need help, shawty?" yelled a neighborhood blockhead.

"Naw, I'm good," she responded as she passed him, walking seductively. She added a little extra in her step because she knew he was watching. "Boy, don't waste your time dreamin' 'bout it"— she paused, turning around to catch the lustful look in his eyes—"'Cuz it's never gonna happen." She winked and continued her stroll to her apartment.

"Man, ain't nobody payin' you no mind," he replied as he cupped his dick and balls. "Wit' yo' half-crazy ass," he mumbled.

"Crazy" was a word she hated. Yvonna contemplated smacking him for the disrespect, but she thought better of it. Instead, she shook her head and cut the corner of the fenced-in entrance. She knew he wanted to fuck her, just like the rest of the hustlers 'round her way.

As her mind wandered, she thought about Cream, one of her best girlfriends. She was mad at her for dropping her off two blocks from her building. If Cream hadn't fucked Yvonna's neighbor's husband, she would've been able to drop her off out front.

But Treyana swore that if she saw Cream anywhere near her block, she'd stomp a mud hole in her ass. And since Treyana had six brothers and sisters, Cream knew Treyana meant it. She didn't stop at just fucking him, she went as far as to shack up with his bum ass in a run-down motel off New York Avenue in D.C. Best believe the dogs were called out on her, so Cream hid out.

When Yvonna reached the apartment building she shared with her six-year-old sister and, as she would say, her senile veteran father, she managed to free three fingers to grab the building's door. Once inside, she cracked it open, stuck her foot in to hold it steady, and twirled her body inside. The glass door bounced on her ass once before she took two steps forward and allowed it to close fully behind her. She briefly placed the bags on the floor to catch her breath and looked up at the two flights of stairs she had to tackle before *finally* getting some rest.

"Damn! Maybe I should've let his ass help!" she said out loud.

Picking the bags back up, she forced herself up the dimly lit hallway. She smiled when she saw her door, realizing in a minute she'd be able to get naked, sit on the couch, and munch on the oatmeal crème pies she had in one of the bags.

Now upstairs, Yvonna placed the bags on the floor and reached for the keys in her pocket. Before letting herself in, she dug in her ass and adjusted the thong, which had been holding her hostage for the past few minutes. So caught up in bullshit, she hadn't heard or sensed the person in the dark hallway behind her.

"Don't scream," he whispered heavily in her

ear as he placed his left hand firmly against her mouth. Yvonna could smell the faint scent of cocoa butter, since his index finger was directly under her nose. "You fuckin' hear me?"

She nodded her head yes.

"Open the door."

It took her a minute to find the right key on the Burberry key chain. The jingling sound resonated in the hallway. When she located the key, she did as instructed and allowed him in as she wrestled with the bags.

"Hurry the fuck up!" he whispered again.

With the bags against the living-room wall, they walked in and he locked the door behind them.

The apartment was totally dark, with the exception of the light that illuminated from the huge fish tank against the living-room wall. Just as she expected, her six-year-old sister, Jesse, was asleep; and she saw no signs of her father.

With his hand still over her mouth, he mumbled, "Now walk over to the couch! You betta not scream. You hear me?"

She nodded yes. When she reached the couch, she bent over the edge, as he demanded. With her ass in the air, and her knees slightly bent, he reveled in her sexiness. The red Baby Phat shorts looked as if they were painted on. Still, they were in the way for what he had planned. With that, he tugged at them until they hung loosely at her ankles.

"Dayyyuummm!" he said, focusing on her honey brown ass in the purple thong. Then he ripped that off too. Yvonna squinted in pain, because the thong had rubbed her raw.

"Don't hurt me," she begged, looking back at him. "I'll do anything you say. Just, please, don't hurt me."

"Didn't I tell you not to say shit?" he asked as he pressed up against her back to reach her ear. He placed more force on her than necessary.

She nodded yes.

"Then why da fuck you speakin'?" Sprinkles of spit touched her face.

She didn't respond.

"Don't say shit else!" he said as he busied himself with the pussy he was about to take.

As he captured her silence, he entered her raw. His dick had grown to a solid seven inches. He was so hard that if he'd been any harder, it would've felt like a bat going in and out of her tiny body. The veins on his dick were pulsating as he fucked her without remorse—not caring about what she was feeling. Licking his lips, he caught a brief glimpse of his balls slapping against her phat ass. When he realized he was being turned on even more, and on the verge of cumming before he wanted to, he allowed her ass cheeks to drop against his stomach. With one hand pressing on the small of her back to keep the arch, he grabbed her hair and used it as a rein to ride her from behind.

"Shit! I'm 'bout to cum!" He moaned. He had her in the perfect position and could no longer hold out.

Hearing this, Yvonna decided there was no way she was about to be left hanging. She slyly backed up into him and twirled her hips with each motion he made. But when she did, he was brought closer to his point.

"I'm about to cummm! Shit!" he yelled.

"Shh!" she managed to answer, thinking her little sister might overhear them.

"Fuck that," he responded. "Your pussy shouldn't be so good."

Yvonna didn't care what he did now. While he was yapping off at the mouth, she'd already gushed her wetness all over his dick. Unlike him, she was able to moan hers out, giving off the impression that she hadn't cum.

"Stay right there," he informed her. "Don't move!"

When he took his slippery dick out, and aimed for her back to release his cum, it reached the glass coffee table, instead. Yvonna burst out into laughter, seeing the mess he'd made. He chuckled and fell into her, his cold platinum diamond chain pressed against her skin.

"You know you crazy, right?" he asked, sounding out of breath.

"I'm crazy? How you figure?"

"'Cuz you stay likin' this rough shit," he replied before pulling up his True Religion jeans.

He then disappeared into the darkness of the apartment and returned with a warm washcloth.

"And you love that I like it rough. Anyway, I thought you couldn't come over tonight," she responded as she rose so he could clean both of their wetness from her body. When he rubbed her exposed vagina with the washcloth, she tensed up due to the rawness she felt.

On the sly, he stuck his finger inside her. "Damn! You still wet! Let me hit it again real quick!" He reached for himself.

"Stop, boy!" She snatched the washcloth from him and cleaned the mess off the table. "I'm already in pain, messin' wit' yo' silly ass!" She slid back into her shorts, leaving the zipper open so her tiny belly could breathe. She didn't see her panties and wasn't searching for them either. She flipped on the kitchen light. "And put them groceries on the counter." She continued talking as her tiny feet slapped against the cold hardwood floor. "Might as well make yourself useful."

Yvonna wondered why he popped up the way that he did. "I thought you were goin' to the party tonight." She grabbed the black rubber hair band that she kept on her arm, and pulled her hair into a ponytail, which sat on the top of her head. "You act like you ain't have no time for me earlier when I called."

"I always got time for you." He pinched her ass.

"Move, boy!" she yelled, secretly loving his aggression. "And how you know what time I was gonna be home?"

"I waited on you. Plus you always go to the store at night. You betta switch your routine up."

"I ain't changin' shit! I hate waitin' in dem long-ass lines. At night I'm in and out. And don't try to skip the subject, B. What's up wit' the party?"

"I'm still goin'." He placed the bags on the counter and looked as if he had something on his mind. "I just came to check you before I left. Plus I wanna talk to you about somethin'."

"Everything okay? Besides the fact that you're standin' me up for the movies again?"

"I'll make it up to you, shawty."

"Oh, I know that," she said, curling her lips. "But you betta know it too!"

He walked up behind her and placed his arms around her waist. The diamond-studded belly ring she wore scratched his arm lightly.

"So you really gonna do it, huh?"

"Yes, Bilal," she responded, stealing a piece of his apple, which he'd taken from the grocery bag. She already knew what he was talking about. Her transporting drugs from D.C. to New York for the gang he belonged to. "And don't start with me . . . because I don't want to hear it."

"What if I tell you I don't want you doin' it? Then what?"

"We already talked about this, Lal!"

"I know we talked about it," he said as a look of concern overtook him. "But I don't think you should do it. Once you get involved in this shit, you stuck."

Yvonna stopped what she was doing and looked into his eyes. His long eyelashes added softness to his rugged features. His black and Spanish heritage made him look exotic. And because he stayed in the streets, the sun caused his skin to bronze.

To hear Yvonna tell it, everything about him was perfect: from his six-foot-two height, to his large dick. And no matter how much he loved wearing plain white T-shirts, baggy jeans, and Nike boots, he still looked like a model with a thuggish quality. He was tatted up. His favorite was the one on his arm that read *LalVon* inside a coffin. It represented his motto that it would be Bilal and Yvonna—the two of them together—till death.

"I hear you, Bilal." She smiled, walking over to him before stealing a passionate kiss. She then ran her hand over his silky goatee. "But I'm a big girl and I been wantin' to get with the Young Black Millionarz before I met you in high school. You act like I'm an angel or somethin'."

"Oh, I know you be throwin' them bows." He chuckled. "That's one of the reasons I love you." He looked into her hazel brown eyes.

"But shit has changed with the YBM. It ain't how it used to be," Bilal cautioned. "Ever since

Crazy Dave and his stepbrother Swoopes got put on, niggas been lunchin' out. Some dudes doin' stuff we ain't used to do. Like stickin' up motha-fuckas and shit. They fucked up all the game."

"Why they even let them in?" she questioned.

"Because they thorough and don't give a fuck," he advised. "And you need a few niggas like that on the squad."

"I don't know 'bout Swoopes, but I think Dave's a punk for real," Yvonna said, fanning her hand in the air. She hated his fucking guts. "Plus I don't appreciate him telling people Sabrina's pussy smelled like cat piss. It ain't like he fucked her! So how would he know, anyway?"

"How you know he ain't hit?"

"I *don't* know." She removed the black shirt she was wearing and allowed her titties to show. She hated clothes. "But he don't eitha."

"No lie—your girl do need a lesson in hygiene." He laughed, pinching her nipples.

"And how do you know?" She hit him on the hand. "Don't be talkin' about her. That's my friend!"

"Everybody know that girl's pussy stink! Every time she get out a car, niggas turn the other way. I mean, she a big girl and all, but she still can wash her ass. That's ree-dic-ulous!"

Yvonna couldn't say much; because although Sabrina was one of her best friends, Yvonna knew what Bilal was saying was true. On many occasions she pulled her to the side to have a conversation with her about her odor, and she still couldn't get it right. Most women wouldn't have the heart to tell their friends, but Yvonna did. She felt sorry for the nigga who fucked and got her pregnant.

They were still talking when Bilal's cell phone rang.

"Hello," he said, walking away from her. He looked back to see if she was watching. She was. "I can't hear you." He said as he walked farther away. He was trying to space himself away from Yvonna, since she was always sweating him about his calls.

Picking up on the cue, Yvonna walked back into the kitchen. *Why the fuck he got to go in the other room?* she thought. *I hope he ain't fuckin' around on me again!*

Bilal was a good dude. However, just like most, he made the mistake of stepping out on her every now and again. And ever since the last time, Yvonna didn't trust him. It didn't make her feel any better that he wasn't with the Young Black Millionarz right now, and he was at her house. It didn't help that he slept over there almost every night, despite living on the Maryland side of town. In her book: once a cheat, always a cheat. Still, love wouldn't allow her to leave him alone.

"Who dat?" she asked, walking up to him

while he was in the living room on the couch. She could no longer bite her tongue.

"I'ma hit you later, man," he said as he ended the call. He didn't want her going off like she had many times in the past. Yvonna had a temper so bad that when she got angry, she would get violent and not remember doing it.

"Bilal, who the fuck was that?" she yelled as she took the black New York Yankees cap off his head and hit him with it.

"Stop trippin', girl!"

"Don't tell me to stop trippin'!" she yelled as she snatched the BlackBerry off his hip and hit send to connect to the last caller. Bilal tried to get ahold of her, but she was too quick. When the phone rang and someone answered, she asked, "Who's this?"

"Why you got his phone?"

When she realized it was a *he,* she suddenly felt stupid for violating Bilal's privacy.

"Oh . . . ," she said, feeling slightly dumb. "It's *just* you."

"Yeah, it's me," Dave responded, irritated. "Why you bein' pressed?"

"Give me my phone, girl," Bilal said, snatching the BlackBerry from her. "How you feel now? Stupid?"

Silence.

"Hello," Bilal said, placing the phone back on his ear.

"You gotta get your girl in check, man. She can't be goin' through your shit."

"Don't worry about me, partna!" He smiled. "I got this over here."

"No, you don't!" Yvonna yelled, still up in his biz.

"I hope you're not serious about what you gonna do either," Crazy Dave said, reminding him of their last conversation. "Real niggas don't go out like that."

"I *am* serious, and just 'cuz I know what I want, don't mean I'm not real."

"Yeah, a'ight, man!" He laughed. "You betta hope she don't find out, 'cuz marrying her ain't gonna change the fact that shawty on the way."

Bilal looked at Yvonna, hoping she couldn't hear what Dave said.

"Like I said, let me do me, and you do you."

"Yeah, whateva. Don't forget 'bout dem dudes neitha. Swoopes owe a lot of money to some cats, and that'll be enough to settle all debts."

"I told y'all, I ain't wit' that shit." He was mad he brought it up.

"Nigga, ain't nobody sayin' you got to do shit." Dave felt Bilal was being soft and his voice was as deep as Method Man's when he addressed him. "But you the only one they trust. You get 'em to the club, and me and Swoopes will do the rest."

"What I tell you 'bout talkin' 'bout this shit over the phone?"

"Yeah, whateva, nigga," Dave replied. "Just don't try and back out."

After he hung up, Bilal placed his phone in his pocket, instead of the clip. He had a few females whom he hadn't fucked in a while lingering around, but nothing serious. Sitting down on the couch, he removed his boots as if nothing had happened.

"Where my slippers, ma?"

"Fuck dem slippers." She frowned. "What his hatin' ass say, 'cause I know he was talkin' 'bout me?" She plopped on the couch next to him, and his hand fondled her breasts. "You know you wanna fuck me, right?"

"Did he tell you that shit?" he asked like he was on his way to confront him. Sitting up straight, he awaited her answer.

"No . . . I can just tell. Whenever he come around, he got to say somethin' to me—even if I ain't speakin' to him."

"You be on his shit too. Don't get dude fucked-up. Dave ain't tryin' to get at you. He just not used to girls speakin' their minds. But I'ma need you to stop clockin' my calls, Yvonna. That shit ain't cool no more. We ain't kids."

"Fuck that!" Yvonna said, slapping his hands off her. "You just betta not be cheatin' again, Bilal. 'Cuz dis time I'm leavin' you!"

"Stop comin' for my head 'bout dat cheatin' shit! You know I ain't fuckin' you over no more."

"Well, you did! You fucked me up, 'cuz I would've never thought you'd step out on me."

Bilal sighed. Once a week he had to prove to her that he was a changed man.

"I don't wanna talk 'bout that shit no more, Yvonna! You can't be monitorin' my phone calls and shit. It's bad for bizness."

"As long as we're together," she responded, reaching for his phone—only to realize it wasn't on his hip. "Nothing's off limit."

With that, she went for his pockets. He didn't fight. Instead of grabbing his phone, she felt a tiny velvet box. As she pulled it out, her eyes got as big as saucers. When she opened it, a diamond solitaire ring stared at her. Without waiting, Bilal got on one knee as she began to fan herself anxiously with her hands.

Taking the box from her, he said, "Yvonna, I fuck wit' . . . I mean"—he paused, clearing his throat and trying to avoid using slang—"I love you. You're the only shawty I can see spendin' the rest of my life with. And I'm bein' real when I say that. I can have fun wit' you, ride or die wit' you—and most of all, I can see havin' kids wit' you. There's nobody out here for me but you."

"Bilal, I can't believe—"

"Don't say nothin', baby," he said, rubbing the tears from her eyes. "When I see how you look afta your sister—despite your father being fucked-up—I smile because I know you would

291

hold me down if shit got rough. We got each otha, and that's real. I don't care what people say 'bout you, or 'bout us bein' together. Everything I do is for you.

"You a dime, Yvonna. You fuck me like I like to be fucked. You can cook your ass off, and you understand the game I'm in and respect it. Fuck dem hatin' mothafuckas out there! I know what I want, and what I want for the rest of my life is you. So what I'm askin' you, baby, is . . . will you do me the honor of being my wife?"

Yvonna jumped up and down and kissed him on every inch of his face before she mumbled what appeared to be a "yes." As she thought about their new life together, she also thought about all the bullshit she went through to get to this point: the cheating, the late-night calls on his cell phone, and the nights she went looking for him—only to find him with another girl.

Bilal stayed fucking around on her in the beginning; but no matter what, he always let it be known that he wasn't leaving her for another bitch. There were females who tried to get him to change his mind, and one in particular took it all the way by telling Yvonna about it. Bilal was known as a "ruthless mothafucka" with manners. He took it as far as it needed to be took, and no further. If he was coming for you, you'd know why; and that was a turn-on for a lot of the chickenheads around the neighborhood.

After Yvonna fucked up the female who told her about Bilal, she approached him about it. And instead of him being a punk, he manned up and told her the truth. But Yvonna wasn't a slouch, and she didn't forgive easily. For six months she cut his ass off. She drove him crazy—not accepting his calls or visits. Little did he know, she was hurting as much as he was. But she decided that she wouldn't take him back until she made him sweat.

That's when she started dating this nigga named Lucy. He was known around the way for being a player. She had the neighborhood buzzing when word got out that the LL Cool J look-alike wanted to give up everything for Yvonna. When Bilal found out, he stepped to them both at Jasper's restaurant. Because Lucy wasn't no busta-ass nigga, Yvonna knew that Bilal was ready for war; and most of all, he was ready to die for her. At that time she missed him so much that she stopped the games and walked out with Bilal, leaving Lucy behind.

"So what up, ma?" he responded as she continued to bombard him with kisses. "You gonna marry me or what?"

"Yes! Yes! Yes! You know I'ma fuckin' marry you!"

"I wanna tell your father," he said, standing up and moving to his room. In all this time he

had never gotten to meet him. "I need his blessing."

"No!" She jumped up. "He'll find out soon
enough."

"Why you don't want me to meet the man?
We been kickin' it for three years and you *still*
don't want me to meet him. Why?"

"You marryin' *me,* so that's all that matters,"
she said, kissing him again. She *really* didn't
want her father embarrassing her. Ever since
he'd been back from the war, he hadn't been
the same.

Needless to say, Bilal didn't leave her that
night. Like always, they crawled in the bed that
Yvonna shared with her six-year-old sister, Jesse.
One of the things Yvonna hated about the
apartment was not having her own space. She
knew Jesse was just as frustrated.

Needing a bigger place was one of the main
reasons Yvonna wanted to get with YBM. She
needed the cash to get Jesse and herself out of
the two-bedroom apartment and into something bigger, without her father. But now it
looked as if the three of them would be a happy
family.

"I love you," Yvonna said as she lay on her
side, and turned her head to kiss Bilal, who was
behind her holding her tight.

"I love you too, ma."

When she looked at Jesse, she smiled when
she saw her sleeping heavily in front of her. She

thanked God for finally bringing her closer to something she always wanted, a family of her own. What she didn't say out loud was that something told her that the happiness wouldn't last.